PERIL IN PERSIA

JUDITH CRANSWICK

© Judith Cranswick 2022
The moral right of the author has been asserted.

All rights reserved. No part of this publication may be reproduced, stored on a retrieval system, or transmitted in any form or by any means, without prior permission of the publisher.

All the characters and institutions in this publication are fictitious. Any resemblance to real persons, living or dead, is purely coincidental.

Published by Liden Press

www.judithcranswick.co.uk

Also by Judith Cranswick

The Aunt Jessica Mysteries
Murder in Morocco
Undercover Geisha

The Fiona Mason Mysteries
Blood on the Bulb Fields
Blood in the Wine
Blood and Chocolate
Blood Hits the Wall
Blood Across the Divide
Blood Flows South
Blood Follows Jane Austen

All in the Mind
Watcher in the Shadows
A Death too Far

Nonfiction

Fun Creative Writing Workshops for the New Writer

PROLOGUE

June 1978

Sheri elbowed her way through the crowd spilling out of the tube station at Earl's Court Road and turned right. The restaurant was no more than three hundred yards but by the time she'd zig-zagged between all the slower moving pedestrians, she was breathing heavily.

A group of boisterous Iranian students stood in the doorway. Before she was tempted to risk their abuse as she tried to push her way through, they headed inside and made for the stairs down to the restaurant-cum-night club in the basement.

The ground floor café was almost empty, and Pamela was chatting with a couple of the other waitresses over by the counter. The tall, lithe New Zealander may not have been the prettiest girl in the place – the Persian dancers who provided the entertainment in the nightclub below were stunning – but she had an enviable figure.

'Pamela,' Sheri called urgently.

The girl looked up and her ready smile quickly turned to a frown. 'What's wrong?'

'Has Mahmoud been in today?'

Pamela shook her head. 'He was here with Hossein yesterday lunch-time, but I haven't seen him since. Why? What's the problem?'

'He's disappeared. We were supposed to be meeting after lectures, but he never showed up. He wasn't in his flat either. I've been looking for him everywhere. I know something bad has happened…'

Pamela held up a hand. 'Whoa there. Slow down, honey. Look, I can see you're upset.'

'But…'

'How's about you and I go and sit down, and you can tell me all about it.'

With a hand under her elbow, Pamela gently but firmly guided the distraught girl to a table in the far corner. 'You make yourself comfy while I get us both a drink.'

Sheri brushed away the tears with the back of her hand then pulled a paper napkin from the metal holder in the centre of the table and blew her nose. By the time Pamela had returned with two glasses of tea from the samovar, she was feeling calmer.

'There's only a few customers in at the moment and the other girls can see to them for a bit. So, tell me what's happened.'

'We arranged to meet up after his three o'clock lecture. I was a bit late getting there. My tutorial with Dr Edwards went on later than I expected. Stupid man wasn't happy with my last essay. Anyway, I waited in the refectory for half an hour. When Mahmoud didn't show, I assumed he'd gone back to his place, so I went round to the house. No one answered when I rang, but I knew at least one of the students was in because as I started to walk away, I saw the curtains twitch in one of the upstairs windows.'

'What did you do then?'

'Went straight back and banged on the door. When they still refused to answer, I screamed through the letterbox that I wasn't going away until someone came to the door.'

Pamela's lips twitched.

'It wasn't funny, I can tell you.'

'No.' Pamela did her best to look contrite. 'What happened next?'

'Eventually that horrible Reza opened the door and shouted at me. That man has had it in for me ever since Mahmoud and I started seeing each other. When I demanded to see Mahmoud, he gave me that disdainful sneer of his and said…' Her voice broke. She took a deep breath before continuing, 'He called me a western slut, no better than an alley cat on heat.'

The tears began to fall, and her shoulders heaved as she gave a loud sob. She pulled more paper napkins from the holder.

Pamela pushed back her chair and crouched down beside the distraught girl, wrapping her arms around her.

Once the crying died down, Sheri continued, 'He said didn't I realised that upper-class Persians like Mahmoud would never be seriously interested in English girls like me who were only too quick to offer themselves to any good-looking man. Mahmoud had been stringing me along and I would never see him again anyway because he'd gone back to Iran.'

'Reza is a nasty piece of work. You should steer clear of him.'

'But Mahmoud's not like that, he's just not. We were planning on getting married as soon as we both graduated next summer.' Pamela frowned, but Sheri rushed on, 'He was coming with me this weekend, to my parents. He was going to ask my father for permission before we went to choose the ring.'

Pamela sat back on her heels, a deep frown on her face.

'You know something don't you?'

Pamela licked her lips, stood up and moved back to her chair.

'What is it? Tell me!'

'The thing is, I've heard rumours. You know as well as I do that some of the Iranian guys have been giving Mahmoud a hard time for weeks, but when it came out that the two of you might be getting engaged… Well, let's just say, things became nasty.'

'You think they've threatened him? Do you know where he is?'

'I've no idea about that.' Pamela backtracked quickly.

'But… I heard a group of them talking yesterday. Did you know Mahmoud had a fiancée back in Iran?'

'He said his family had chosen a wife for him when he was still a child. She's the daughter of a distant cousin. His own family may be part of what passes for minor aristocracy, but they don't have a great deal of money and this girl's dowry would make a big difference to the family's future. That's why he was going to get a job in England once he'd qualified so he didn't have to return.'

'If you say so.' Pamela gave a weak smile.

'Are you saying he was lying to me? I'll have you know…'

'That's not what I meant.' Pamela put up her hands to ward off the waves of anger flooding across the table. 'You don't have to convince me that he wants to marry you.'

'Then what do you mean? You know something, don't you? What are you not telling me?'

Pamela dropped her gaze to her hands resting on the table. 'I just work here. I pick up things. I heard some of the students talking about how determined he is to stay in England and how once he was married, he'd be entitled to a British passport and couldn't be forced to return to Iran. I'm not saying I believe them, mind. I'm sure he really loves you just as much as you love him.'

'Of course he does,' Sheri snapped back. 'Besides, if all he wanted was a British passport he wouldn't be missing now, would he?'

'I think you should talk with Hossein. He is Mahmoud's best buddy. He may be able to tell you more. If anything has happened to Mahmoud, he might know.'

Sheri sighed. 'They might be mates, but I'm not sure he approves of me.'

'Your choice. In any case, you making a scene outside their house isn't going to help anyone. Least of all Mahmoud. He won't thank you for it.'

'So, what can I do?'

Pamela shrugged.

'All I'm saying is you can't trust Reza. You've heard the rumours.'

'But he wouldn't hurt Mahmoud. They're second cousins for goodness' sake.'

'Maybe not. But as you said, Mahmoud's family are not flush with money. He's only able to study over here at all because of the grant. One whiff of scandal and he could lose it. And, just because the two of them are related, Reza might see it as his duty to make sure Mahmoud is forced to return to Iran to marry this girl to maintain the family honour.'

Sheri slumped forward and buried her head in her arms.

Pamela tentatively put a hand on the sobbing girl's shoulder. 'I'm so, so sorry.'

CHAPTER 1

October Present Day

I've never liked hospitals. Even as a visitor, they make me nervous. I clutched the cake tin to my chest and followed my mother along the echoing corridors. The occasional skeletal metal bed with its thin plastic mattress pushed against the wall only added to my unease at what lay ahead. With each step, the tension began to build across the back of my shoulders travelling down my arms until my fingers suddenly became rigid.

'Come along, Harry. Hickling Ward is just along here. Third doorway on the right.'

I dutifully trailed in her footsteps, reading the overhead signs all named after one of the Norfolk Broads. By the time I caught up, she'd already used the hand-sanitiser and gone inside.

For some reason, the contraption didn't seem to want to work for me. I looked around but there was nowhere to rest the tin, so I put it on the floor and tried again. I kept pressing the dispenser button, but nothing happened. Suddenly, it spat a whole stream of sticky liquid into my waiting palm. After wringing my hands in vain, I was tempted to wipe the surplus on the back of my trousers until one of the nurses glared at me as though reading my thoughts. I picked up my tin and scurried quickly after my mother.

She was already at the far end of the ward. The figure in the bed turned as I approached.

My mother had warned me that my aunt had lost weight since the fall which had resulted in a broken hip, but could that frail-looking, hollow-cheeked figure really be my fearsome Aunt Maud, the scourge of my life who had terrified me ever since I was a toddler?

I stopped stock-still, still clutching the tin I'd been so carefully carrying from the car park. The smile I'd previously plastered on my face must have fallen because the pale gimlet eyes narrowed as she snapped, 'I'm not dead yet.'

I bent to kiss the paper-thin skin of her cheek desperately trying to think of something to say.

'You'd better fetch yourself a chair. There's a stack of them by the door, but before you do, pull that curtain across and give us at least the illusion of a little more privacy.'

By the time I'd returned from doing my aunt's bidding, my mother was chattering away nineteen to the dozen. '...When they arrived home from the hospital this morning, Edwina and Jessica said how much brighter you were today, and I must say you have a lot more colour than yesterday.'

As I went to put the chair alongside my mother's, Aunt Maud shook her head and patted the other side of the bed. 'Come and sit here next to me, young man. It was good of you to drive Jessica up from London, yesterday.'

'I came because *I* wanted to see how you are.'

She raised an imperious eyebrow and the thin lips twitched. She may have lost a great deal of the old vigour but the gleam in those pale grey eyes was in no way diminished.

'I did!' I protested.

'If you say so. Is this for me?'

She tapped the lid of the tin I'd placed on the bed when I'd gone to get the chair.

'As Aunt Jessica brought you a fruit basket this morning, I thought I'd make you some biscuits.'

'Still playing chef I see.'

She moved the tin onto her lap, prised open the lid and peered in at the contents. 'What are they?'

'Oat, fruit and nut clusters. Mum said you weren't too fond of hospital food and I thought they'd be quite nourishing. They're full of protein.'

Her expression didn't inspire confidence, but she thanked me and told me to put them in the bedside locker. I wondered as I knelt down if they'd ever get eaten, though to do her justice, the huge fruit basket on the top had left little room for anything else.

It was stiflingly hot in the ward which didn't add to my comfort levels. I removed my jacket and hung it over the chair.

My mother filled the hiatus. 'Talking of food, did you eat a proper lunch?'

'The shepherd's pie they served up was unpalatable. Hardly any lamb and the mashed potato was so watery it collapsed into a soggy mess covering the whole plate.'

My mother shook her head. 'The sooner we can get you home and start feeding you up again, the better. Aren't the medical staff concerned about the amount of weight you've lost?'

'Stop fussing, Constance. Apparently, it's quite normal for patients to lose a few pounds when they come in. Something to do with the body's response to shock. Besides, when I first came in, I was told by one young doctor that I was grossly overweight which is why I did so much damage when I fell.'

My mother gave an angry snort while I quickly hid the involuntary smile as I thought of the likely retort Aunt Maud would have given him. Not that it was a laughing matter, but I'd lay odds that the doctor would choose his words more carefully when he spoke to her in future.

As my mother quickly changed the subject by passing on the good wishes sent by the village WI ladies hoping for Aunt Maud's recovery, I resumed my seat.

It was only a minute or so before my aunt turned back to me.

'Your mother said you've moved out of Jessica's flat at last and into your own place.'

'It's more of a glorified bed-sit really.' Why was I apologising? I should be proud of myself for what I'd achieved in the last year. Thanks to Aunt Jessica, I'd gone from a pathetic out-of-work no-hoper to an up-and-coming business entrepreneur. I might still have a long way to go but it was time to stop caving in to Aunt Maud's constant put-downs.

'Properties in London must be very expensive.'

'Absolutely. But now the business is beginning to take off, I can afford my own place.' No need to explain it had only one decent-sized room which I use as my office partitioned off from the kitchen-cum-diner, a tiny box bedroom plus a separate shower room.

She still looked sceptical, so before she could start implying it was in some tatty backstreet, I hurried on, 'It's only ten minutes on the tube from Aunt Jessica's, so I still pop back regularly. She's very fond of my Sunday roasts and I make a mean treacle pud.'

'She said this morning how much she misses your cooking.'

'Aunt Jessica may have been one of the leading archaeologists in her field before she retired, but let's just say her talents lie outside the kitchen.'

My mother laughed but Aunt Maud still looked frosty.

'So, you are doing well with your latest enterprise, I take it?'

I was beginning to falter, but I forced myself to brave it out. 'Inevitably it takes time to build up a reputation for any new undertaking, but so far, I've managed to hit all the predicted targets on my business plan.'

'That's something I suppose. And you're keeping up with the bank repayments?'

'Absolutely.' I nodded vigorously.

Probably best not to tell her that it was only thanks to the frequent staff cover sessions I did at Mario's Trattoria where I'd worked as a temporary chef for three months earlier in the year. And definitely not that I still owed Aunt Jessica a hefty sum in back-rent for the ten months she'd put me up, the repayment on the sizable loan for the three-month advanced rent on my flat plus the down payment on all the equipment for my new IT consultancy business.

'He was telling me in the car on the way over that he's signed up three more clients this last fortnight. They want him to design new websites for them,' interrupted my mother, keen as always to jump my defence.

After half an hour, even my mother was running out of things to say so the arrival of the tea trolley provided a welcome distraction. Cups of tea were strictly for the patients but judging from the colour of the pale liquid that slopped into the saucer as it was banged down on the table at the end of the bed, I doubt there was more than a single tea bag per half dozen cups.

'Sugar?'

'No thank you,' my aunt replied tartly as the morose woman went on her way.

'That's not the usual tea lady, is it?' said my mother. 'I've not seen her before.'

'No. It's her day off. Some of these relief workers leave a lot to be desired.'

'Let me get that for you.' I moved my chair out of the way and wheeled the table further up the bed so Aunt Maud could reach it.

'Why don't you rescue your biscuits from the locker, Harry? I'm sure your aunt would love one with her tea, wouldn't you dear?'

To my surprise, Aunt Maud acquiesced to my mother's beaming smile. It was easy to assume that my mother – always anxious to please her much older and more assertive sisters – was easily put upon and to forget just how wily she could be when she chose.

As I went to place the tin alongside the cup, my mother leant across and took it from me, removed the lid and held it out to her sister.

Aunt Maud took one and held it between her fingers, staring at it dubiously before taking a small tentative bite.

I held my breath as I waited for the verdict.

'Not bad. Could do with a bit more sugar, but not bad.' She took a larger bite. 'Quite acceptable in fact.'

'I'm glad you like it.'

She picked up her cup, but it dripped across the table.

My mother jumped to her feet. 'I'll go and find a cloth.'

She was halfway down the ward before I had a chance to get to my feet.

A surprisingly strong hand gripped my arm holding me back. 'Let her go. It will give us a chance to talk properly.'

I sank back in my chair.

'So tell me, how is your business really doing? Setting up on your own without any capital behind you sounds a risky undertaking.'

'I was lucky the temporary contract I had at the restaurant came at the right time to sub me while I was building up the business. Things progressed steadily over the first few months till I was able to show the bank I was a viable proposition. They were happy with my business plan and gave me a loan. Not as much as I'd asked for, I'll admit, but still substantial. I can't pretend it's been easy, but so far, I'm keeping my head above water. I'm getting a steady stream of enquiries and enough contracts to keep me busy especially with the new clients who've just come onboard. One's quite small, just a straightforward update on an existing website and ongoing support, but the second one wants lots of fancy animation which will be fun to do. They both came from recommendations by satisfied customers, which is always gratifying. I haven't needed to spend much on advertising so far. Added to my existing contracts, I'll be busy for the next couple of months at least, even if I don't pick up any more in the meantime.'

She took another biscuit before saying, 'I thought your mother said earlier that you had three new clients.'

Trust her to notice.

'I'm still negotiating with someone who's keen to expand her childminding service. It's a project I'd really love to do. To be honest, the last few contracts have only been standard websites, bread-and-butter work, but this would be something I could really get my teeth into.'

'Are you likely to get it?'

I shrugged my shoulders. 'We had a long session together and she's really enthusiastic about my proposals for a complete marketing package, but it's a question of whether she can afford it. I'm in no hurry to rush her. Apart from being busy with my two new clients, there's little point in pushing someone who might default on her payments after I've done much of the work.'

'Very sensible,' my aunt muttered as she selected another biscuit from the tin. I wasn't sure if she was listening to me, but even if it was only a means to keep getting some nourishment into her, my prattle could only be a good thing.

'I can appreciate exactly the position she's in,' I continued. 'She's reached the stage where she knows that if she wants to upgrade a good little earner that's bringing in steady pin money into a proper business, she's going to need to make a big capital investment. She's already looked at a number of companies that offer a similar service to mine, but they are all out of her price range.'

Aunt Maud snapped her head round, eyes flashing, lips pursed. 'She wants you to do it on the cheap?'

'No. Not at all.' So much for my earlier assumption about my aunt's preoccupation with the biscuits! 'She was quite up front about her situation, but once I'd showed her my rough designs for the social media packages and she saw the quality of the photos I'd taken of her facilities, she was really keen. In the end, we agreed to plot out a staggered approach spread over a year. Starting with a basic package, the plan is to upgrade to the next level once the business could afford it. I left her with some idea of my costs for each item – social media design, fliers, brochures, blog, website, and so on. I suggested she take a few weeks to think about it and work out exactly what would be most cost effective to begin with and set out the financial targets to reach her short- and medium-term goals and then get back to me.'

I stopped talking when she suddenly leant back against the pillows and pushed the table further down the bed. 'I think it's time you put the lid back on the tin and tucked it back in the locker.'

'You enjoyed them then?'

She glared at me. 'Did I say that?'

I did as I'd been told. Out of sight, knelt down to find a space in the locker, I couldn't resist a grin.

As I returned to my feet my mother appeared from round the curtain.

'I'm so sorry I've taken so long, Maud. None of the nurses could help me and I had to go all the way down to the ground floor to find someone from the cleaning department.'

'No matter. Your son has kept me amused while you were gone.'

'That's good,' twittered my mother. I caught the half-smile and the knowing gleam in her eye as she busied herself wiping the table. Just how long had she been standing behind that curtain waiting for the right moment to appear? If nothing else this weekend, I was beginning to appreciate a side to the Hamilton women I'd never really taken in before.

'Did Jessica tell you about all the places she and Harry will be going to on the trip? Those photos on her tablet of some of those elaborate mosques were quite stunning.'

'She did. Though why she is so enthusiastic at the prospect of returning to such a benighted country, beats me. Beautiful it may be, but it seems foolhardy to allow tourists to visit a country where its leaders appear to want to wage war against the rest of the world.'

The cheerful mask on my mother's face dropped momentarily revealing the deep-seated fears she shared with her more forthright sister.

'We're going with a reputable company who've been doing this same trip for years. They would hardly risk their reputation if there was the faintest hint of danger.'

It was an old argument and one my mother knew she could never win. 'You must promise me you'll take care, Harry.'

'Yes, Mother.'

'And don't eat the salads. And make sure everything you eat is piping hot. You never know in these backward countries.'

'We'll be staying in luxury hotels. There's no need to worry. Anyway,' I glanced at Aunt Maud who was lying back on her pillows with her eyes closed. 'I think it's time we both left you to get some rest, Aunt. You must be quite tired after all the visitors you've had today.'

She opened her eyes and glared at me. 'Don't patronise me, young man. When are you going back to London?'

'Probably first thing tomorrow.'

My mother gave a heartfelt sigh. 'It's such a pity you couldn't stay a couple more days.'

'The plane leaves the next day and there's still lots of last-minute things to do before we leave. The taxi is picking us up at half-twelve on Sunday to take us to Heathrow.'

I stood up and took my jacket from the back of the chair.

'I know,' said my mother. 'But Maud is coming home on Tuesday. It would have been so nice if you'd still been here.'

'So soon! I didn't realise. But will you be able to cope?'

'Of course we will,' Aunt Maud snapped. 'There's no

need to fuss. You're as bad as your mother.'

I picked up my chair. 'I'll just return this to where it came from.'

My brain was in overdrive. Even though she'd lost weight, she was still a big woman. Far too heavy for two elderly ladies to help in and out of bed, never mind coping getting up and down the stairs. By the time I'd returned, I'd made a decision.

'Change of plan. I'll drive Aunt Jessica back as arranged but I'll be back. Once I've shown her exactly how to use the digital projector for her talks, I'm convinced she'll be able to manage. She doesn't really need me. If she has any problems, I'm sure there'll be plenty of tech savvy people around who can help.' I turned to Aunt Maud. 'I'll be back in plenty of time to drive you home from the hospital.'

'Stop right there, young man. If you think I'm going to let you...'

I put up a hand and stopped her mid-flow. 'When you get back, you are going to need help getting around. I am well aware you consider me a complete waste of space and a disgrace to the family name, but in this instance, you have no choice. Apart from anything else, I refuse to let you put the burden of your care onto the shoulders of my mother and Aunt Edwina. They are both too old to take on that responsibility.'

'Harry! You can't speak to Maud like that.'

'I'm sorry, Mum, but it has to be said.'

When I turned back to Aunt Maud, far from being puce with rage at my impudence, there was a hint of a smile at the corners of her mouth.

'If you would let me finish,' she said calmly, 'I was going to say that I've no intention of letting you miss out on this trip. Jessica says that since you started this consultancy of yours, you have worked every hour there is. You deserve this break, so off with you and enjoy a well-deserved holiday.'

To say I was taken aback by her reaction was something

of an understatement. In all my thirty-five years, this was the first time I could remember that she'd ever had anything remotely good to say about me. 'That's as maybe,' I said with less conviction. 'But there is a matter of mobility. How are you going to get up and down stairs without help?'

'Social services have arranged for a carer to come in to help me getting in and out of bed and washed and dressed. First thing on Monday morning, someone is arriving to assess the house and provide any additional equipment I may need until I'm fully mobile. And as for driving me home, we do have such things as taxis, even in Norfolk.'

'Oh!' I stood there feeling foolish.

'Now be off, the pair of you.'

As I bent to kiss her cheek she said, 'If you want to make it up to me, you can make me another batch of those biscuits before you leave. Only with a few less nuts. They get under my false teeth.'

'Yes, Aunt.'

CHAPTER 2

We set off back to London the next morning a little later than planned. By the time we hit the city outskirts, the traffic was already building up fast.

'We're not going to get back until gone lunch-time at this rate,' I muttered as the white minivan ahead of us stopped when the traffic lights turned red.

'You getting uptight about it won't get us there any quicker,' said Aunt Jessica.

'But I told the hire people I'd get the car back to them by two o'clock. At this rate, by the time I've dropped you off, I'll be lucky to make it.'

She put her hand on my arm. 'They'll be alright, you know.'

I couldn't pretend I didn't know what she was talking about. She knew exactly the real cause of my frustration. I took a deep breath. 'I know, but I still feel guilty, jetting off to enjoy myself.'

'According to Connie, Maud gave you pretty short shrift when you suggested staying behind.'

'You could say that. She's a difficult woman to cross.'

'Maybe, but for all her razor tongue, her heart's in the right place. Your mother said she enjoyed the biscuits you made.'

'You think so?' I caught my scowl in the driving mirror. 'First off, she complained I'd not used enough sugar then she said I'd used too many nuts. She didn't even say thank you.'

Aunt Jessica chuckled. 'But she tucked into them and

asked you to make her some more.'

I gave a long sigh.

'That's just her way. You should be used to it by now.'

The lights changed to green. I put the car into gear and eased forward.

Once we were out of the city limits and on the open road, I began to feel more my normal self. Given that in just over twenty-four hours we'd be on our way to Heathrow airport, it was time to stop worrying about how my mother and her ageing sisters were going to manage and check what still needed to be done to be in readiness for the holiday.

'I can't believe we're off tomorrow. It's come with such a rush,' I said.

'Remind me when you drop me off to check our seat allocations for tomorrow's flights. There's not usually much chance to change, but do you have a preference?'

'Not really. I'd rather not be right at the back next to the loos, but other than that I'm easy. Will the details for the onward flight from Istanbul be up yet?'

'The plane doesn't leave until just after midnight but as it's an onward flight, it might be possible. I'll check the Turkish Airlines website.'

'Okey-dokey.'

'After that, I suppose I'd better ring the company and see if there's been any last-minute changes,' said Aunt Jessica as she rooted in the depths of her bag for her notebook.

'I thought you spoke to someone last Monday.'

She gave an angry snort. 'I did. That's when they told me that the tour guide I've had on all my previous trips is on maternity leave. She was excellent and we got on so well together.'

'I'm sure her replacement will be just as good.'

'Let's hope so.'

'Maybe, but that's not the point. They must have known

Azita wouldn't be available in November months ago, so why did they wait until less than a week before the start of the holiday to let me know? It makes you wonder what else they haven't bothered to tell me.'

She scribbled in her notebook. 'All my notes are in the filing cabinet so that's not a problem, but I need to check what printouts I'm going to need. Now you've put my talks on PowerPoint, there aren't that many, but I will give everyone a list of the passengers and a map showing the itinerary.'

'All I need to do is pack. I've already sorted out things like sunscreen and hand-sanitiser. It shouldn't take too long to throw a few clothes in the holdall. Am I going to need anything special?'

'Long trousers but short-sleeved shirts are fine. Though don't forget to make sure you have socks when you're out each day. If you have to take your shoes off to go into a mosque, it's disrespectful to enter in bare feet.'

'Will do.'

She gave a long sigh. 'You men have it easy. Apart from having to cover our hair with a scarf in public, we have to wear long-sleeved tunics that hide our backsides and trousers that don't show our ankles.'

'Quite right too. Can't have you ladies inflaming men's passions, can we?'

'Chance would be a fine thing at my age!'

'Oh, I don't know. Isn't seventy meant to be the new forty?'

'Cheeky monkey!'

At least I'd made her laugh again.

CHAPTER 3

The big day arrived. Once we'd checked in at the airport, we spent some time wandering round Terminal 2 comparing the various eating places. Neither of us fancied a large lunch and in the end, we settled for a couple of duck-in-hoisin-sauce filled wraps and a coffee. I treated myself to a slice of gooey-looking chocolate cake that turned out to be disappointing.

The flight was scheduled to take off at sixteen-fifty hours. We were half an hour late boarding and despite my aunt's best efforts the day before, our seats were well towards the back of the plane. I spent the first part of the flight reading through the itinerary booklet.

'Our hotel in Tehran sounds extremely grand – "*Located in the historic centre, the Palace hotel provides a haven of luxury in the heart of the busy city*". Does it live up to the company's glowing description? In my limited experience, the hotels in capital cities tend to be somewhat cramped and often part of a characterless chain.'

'Definitely not in this case. It's glitz and glamour personified. You'll be impressed. Miles of marble floors, mosaics on the walls, glittering chandeliers, the works. The manager is a real character. A lovely man, and he adores the English. He always comes to speak to us. He was a student at the London School of Economics back in the late seventies. The last Shah of Iran was very keen to modernise his country and he funded a whole raft of young men to study in Britain. Mr Kamali was one of them. His father-in-law owned a chain of hotels in Tehran which is why he ended up in the industry.'

'I suppose being fluent in English was a great asset.'

'True. English is the second language for so many countries, but he's quite a linguist. He's familiar with a great many languages. I suppose it comes with the job.'

The turnaround time at Istanbul was an hour, but take-off at Heathrow had been delayed. I was relieved to see that as the plane began to make its descent, we'd made up some of the time.

'We don't seem to be anywhere near the stand. It's difficult to tell in the dark, but I can't see any sign of the terminal building.'

Aunt Jessica was still engrossed in her book. I wasn't sure she'd even heard me. Ten minutes later, we didn't seem to be any closer.

'The pilot's taxiing around in circles!'

'Um,' she muttered as she looked up. 'What's the problem?'

'I was only saying we seem to have landed in the middle of nowhere. I'm not sure the pilot has any idea of where he's going. Do you think he's lost?'

She chuckled. 'We've a way to go yet. The landing strip is right at the edge of the airfield.'

'But we'll miss our connection!'

'I expect they'll hold it for us. They know we're coming. Panicking won't make things any quicker.'

A tall man in some sort of uniform was waiting impatiently for us when we eventually disembarked. He'd already collected all the others in our party who I assumed had been seated further to the front of the aircraft. Without bothering to give us any explanation, our guide strode off into the distance and we fell in behind.

'He's taking us to the correct gate,' explained Aunt Jessica.

On the basis that this had happened on one of her earlier trips to Iran, I didn't question her judgement and followed on the tail end of the crocodile forging its way through the crowds. For a seventy-three-year-old woman, my aunt is surprisingly fit – no doubt the result of a lifetime scrabbling about in tricky terrain on remote archaeological digs – and I was the one who was having difficulty keeping up. In addition to a large rucksack on my back, my bulky camera gear strapped across my chest, plus the laptop and projector bags over each shoulder, it was proving a tricky proposition to manoeuvre my way through the mass of people. It didn't help that I found myself stuck behind a wheelchair accompanied by a large family who seemed totally impervious to the fact that I was trying to get past.

Not that I was the only one having problems keeping up. Although a good ten years younger and a good deal shorter and stouter than my aunt, one of the other women was having trouble getting her carry-on suitcase onto the escalator. I stopped to help and had a moment of panic when we reached the top.

'Did you see which way they turned?'

I caught sight of my aunt who had stepped out into a clear space to cut round a family clustered together and barring her way.

'That way,' I shouted over the noise, pointing my companion in the right direction.

She and I were the last to present our boarding cards as the "Gate Closed" notice flashed above the entrance to the ramp down towards the last bus waiting to drive us out to the aircraft.

The flight was only just over three hours. After take-off and the usual serving of a drink and bag of strange nibbles not long after, I put the seat back and closed my eyes. Not that I managed to get any sleep. I was just beginning to doze off when the rumble of the snacks trolley brought me back to full consciousness. There was little point trying to get back to sleep once the rubbish was collected because the air stewards were soon back touting the sale of duty-free goods quickly followed by the dishing out and filling in of necessary entrance forms for foreign nationals.

We landed at four in the morning, but once we'd cleared passport control and reached the arrivals lounge, we had to give our names to the company rep checking our details on his list. Our tour guide was waiting for us a short distance away. Aunt Jessica may have had a few qualms at having a different guide to the one she was used to, but I took to Aahil straight away. He was younger than me, late-twenties, outgoing and strikingly good-looking. The two of us were soon chatting away as we waited for the last of the party to arrive.

'Your English is excellent,' I said.

'Thank you.' Aahil smiled shyly. 'I spent three years in London as a student.'

'Really? I live in London. Which college?'

'Imperial.'

'Very impressive. Did you enjoy living in London?'

'Oh yes. The museums in Knightsbridge were wonderful and there was so much to see – the cathedrals, the Tower of London.'

'Then you probably know it all better than I do. I only recently moved to London, and I still haven't been to St Paul's or the Houses of Parliament yet.' No need to tell him Aunt Jessica had taken pity on me when I was all but destitute and could no longer afford the rent on my flat in Bedford ten months ago.

There was no more time to chat as everyone was now gathered. Aahil led the way outside towards the waiting coach. Despite it being pitch black outside, the path to the coach park was well lit. In addition to my aunt and I, there were ten other passengers.

'Your Mr Kamali isn't the only one who studied in England. So did Aahil,' I said to Aunt Jessica as we waited to get on the coach.

'It didn't take long for you to start chatting up the first good-looking young man. Just remember where you are.'

'We were only talking.'

I took the cases for the driver to load into the luggage compartment while Aunt Jessica boarded the coach.

From the outside, it looked like any other large coach, but at the top of the steps, I paused.

'Goodness me!'

The woman I'd helped with her case at the airport, who was sitting in the front seat, chuckled and said, 'It is a bit different, isn't it?'

The seats were anything but standard. They'd all been replaced with large buckets seats. They took up so much space that on the right side of the aisle, there was only room for a line of single seats. There was so much distance between each row that there could only have been room for half the usual number of passengers.

'This is rather special, isn't it? Just like a first-class seat on a plane,' I said as I slid into the window seat next to Aunt Jessica. I sat back and flipped up the leg support from under my seat. 'Look, even with my legs fully stretched out, my toes still don't reach the seat in front.'

She gave me an indulgent smile.

'What?' I demanded.

'You're like a kid in a sweet shop.'

I grinned back. 'This may be all in a day's work to you, but I'm still not used to jetting off to exotic places. I never left Norfolk till I went to uni and before you took me to Morocco last year, my only foreign travel was a camping holiday in France.'

Once we were all settled, Aahil tapped the mic to get our attention. 'As you have been travelling for a long time, I'm sure you are all feeling quite tired, so I will keep this brief. Let me first introduce you to our driver, Hassan. He is going to be with us for the whole tour. It will take us about twenty minutes to get to your hotel and when we arrive, I will check you all in and once you have your keys, you can go straight to your rooms for a well-earned rest. We will all meet again in the main lobby at midday. Now, if you have all secured your seat belts, we will be off.'

Before we had even driven out of the airport, the guy in the single seat ahead on the other side of the aisle took out his mobile and began tapping.

I nudged my aunt and whispered, 'Who on earth do you think he's phoning at this time of the morning?'

'Perhaps he's sending a text back home to say he's arrived safely.'

'Don't think so. I can't make out what he's saying but he's definitely talking to someone.'

'For goodness' sake, Harry. Behave yourself and stop being such a nosy parker!'

There was no one sitting behind us, so I adjusted the seat and lay back. 'Wake me up when we get there!'

Aunt Jessica sighed and shook her head. I was much too excited to sleep and put my seat back to upright and stared out of the window. I had no intention of missing any of it. Not that I could see much in the dark, but the mosques were all lit up with strings of coloured lights everywhere.

A thought struck me. 'If we have the same driver all the time, does that mean we have the same coach?'

'We do.'

I looked round my seat and did a quick count. Even with the row of only single bucket seats opposite there were still twenty-four seats.

'But it's a full-sized coach and there's only a dozen of us!'

'Iran is a large country, three times the size of France, and believe me you will appreciate it when we have to spend much of the day travelling between sites.'

'But don't we have an internal flight in a couple of days?'

She nodded. 'First thing on Wednesday morning, from Tehran to Kerman. Hassan and his assistant will take it in shifts to drive through the night and they'll meet us at the airport when we land.'

When we reached the hotel, a small army of porters appeared the moment the coach pulled up by the red carpet that led up the steps. Before the last of our small party had descended from the coach, our cases were being whisked away and hurried to our rooms.

The Palace Hotel was everything its name and the glowing writeup in our notes had promised. We were ushered into an enormous marble lobby to wait while Aahil went to check us in.

Aunt Jessica disappeared off to the reception desk to ask where she would be able to give her lectures. The first one was scheduled for when we all met up again at midday. She'd asked me to stay and look after our hand luggage. As that included her laptop and the digital projector, I didn't want to leave it unattended.

I placed the equipment carefully beside one of the armchairs but before I could sit down there was someone beside me.

'Hi, I'm Irene. I never had the chance to say thank you for helping me with my case at the airport in Istanbul.'

'No problem. I'm Harry, by the way.'

'Are you travelling with your mother?'

I shook my head. 'I'm Jessica's nephew. She is the history lecturer.'

'I rather gathered that. I'm really looking forward to her talks. I'd better be getting back, but I just had to come and say how grateful I am. I was panicking a bit that I was going to get left behind until you came along.'

'My pleasure.'

She returned to her seat next to another much younger woman. I couldn't tell the colour of her hair because, like all the women, it was now covered by a long scarf wrapped over her head and shoulders.

This was the first opportunity I'd had to study my fellow passengers. There was only one man on his own, the one

I'd noticed on the coach making a phone call. Now I could see him more clearly and could appreciate his swarthy complexion and Middle Eastern features, I realised whoever he'd been phoning probably wasn't back in England at all. The rest of the party included three married couples – all round about retirement age – plus three other ladies – Irene, the younger woman next to her, and the third was a short, lively woman doing most of the talking with the man with the grey beard and his wife. She seemed to be the only perky one in the party. The others all looked as I felt – dog tired and longing to be allowed to go up to our rooms and get our heads down for a few hours' kip.

I was about to introduce myself to the couple sitting next to me when Aunt Jessica returned accompanied by the manager. At least, as they were chatting away like long lost friends, I presumed it must be the famous Mr Kamali that she'd told me about on the plane. With his rotund figure, bald pate and black upturned waxed moustache, he was a shoo-in for David Suchet's Hercule Poirot though without the mincing walk.

He greeted everyone with a nod and a beaming smile as his eyes scanned round the group, 'Ladies and gentlemen, may I welcome you to the Palace Hotel. I will not keep you after your long journey, but I did want to say, if there is anything we can help you with during your stay, please do not hesitate to let me or one of my staff know.'

As he turned to leave, he suddenly looked back over his shoulder and stared again at someone sitting behind me. He gave a slight frown before walking briskly back the way he'd come.

I twisted in my chair to see who he'd been looking at, but it was impossible to tell.

CHAPTER 4

We were offered breakfast, but most people, including my aunt and me, declined and went straight up to our rooms once we'd been given our key cards.

'Did you have any success finding out where you can give your lecture?' I asked once we'd extracted ourselves from the crowded lift.

'Nothing's been pre-arranged, but Mr Kamali arrived while I was at reception, and he promised to find somewhere suitable by the time we're ready to set up.'

Our main cases had already been delivered and were waiting by our rooms. She opened her door and I followed her in, released the carrying straps and laid her camera gear and the equipment on the table.

'That stuff's heavy,' I said, rubbing my shoulder.

'Why do you think I bring you along?'

I pulled a rude face, and she laughed. 'Very mature!'

'What time do you want to go down for the lecture? Once we know where we're going to be, it won't take long for me to set up for you.'

'Shall we say, quarter to twelve?'

'Fine with me.'

At the door, I turned to ask, 'By the way, did you notice Mr Kamali do a doubletake as he was leaving us? He definitely looked back at one of our group, but I couldn't work out who.'

She shook her head.

'I couldn't quite make out his expression. I'm not sure if he was anxious or puzzled, but I'd swear he'd recognised someone.'

'That doesn't seem very likely.'

'Perhaps it was that Middle Eastern guy.'

'If you say so.' She didn't sound convinced, but it was time to get my head down before what looked like being a busy afternoon with two visits, one to the Crown Jewels Museum and then on to a Glassware and Ceramic Museum.

Everyone seemed to enjoy Aunt Jessica's first talk giving us an introduction to Persia and a general outline of its history. I for one, knew very little about the country. It wasn't until I'd put the slides together using the maps and pictures that she'd given me that I realised just how huge the Empire was. It stretched from Egypt and northern central Greece in the west across Asia to the Indus Valley in the east and was the largest empire the world had seen up to that point.

From the questions afterwards, it seems I wasn't the only one to appreciate the lecture. The first hand to shoot up was the live wire who had come on her own and I now knew was called Barbara.

'I confess my head's spinning with all these different dynasties. Is it possible to have a copy of the slide you showed with the timeline?'

'Don't worry. There's not going to be an exam at the end. By the end of the holiday these names will all fall into place as we visit different parts of the country,' Aunt Jessica reassured her. 'I didn't want to burden you with any handouts today but when we visit the National Museum, you'll have a much better idea of what you're seeing.'

It was easy to gauge from the questions they asked that there were two or three people who were already quite knowledgeable about the country including the guy with the beard and the younger woman, but, like me, the rest appeared to have only a smattering of knowledge.

I noticed Aahil was looking at his watch. Another hand was raised but, before the poor woman had a chance to ask her question, Aahil was on his feet. 'Why don't we continue the discussion over lunch? Many of you must be hungry after skipping breakfast.'

As the others began to file out after him, I began to unplug the projector and coil the cables. Aunt Jessica came to help me.

'I appreciate what you were telling us was familiar to him, but that was a bit abrupt, breaking up the party like that, wasn't it?'

'Don't blame Aahil. I wasn't expecting all those questions and timing is a bit tight. We're already ten minutes later than planned for lunch. He's worried we'll miss our slot at the Crown Jewels Museum. They're pretty strict about timing.'

'I see. You'd better go with everyone else in case they still have questions. You can save me a place while I take this lot upstairs.'

As I stepped out of the lift into the lobby, I realised I wasn't the only one not already at lunch. The man who made those early phone calls on the coach as we first arrived was at the reception desk talking to the young woman on duty. I'd hardly taken a dozen steps when without warning, he banged his fist on the counter and, in a voice that echoed around the vast auditorium, demanded to speak to the manager. Feeling like a startled rabbit suddenly caught in car headlights, I froze. The last thing I wanted was to appear to be trying to listen in, so I scuttled behind a pillar.

I was still debating whether to retreat the short distance back to the lift and try to find another way to get to the restaurant or to brazen it out and cross the wide expanse where I could not fail to be observed by anyone glancing in that direction, when Mr Kamali appeared. Presumably he'd heard the commotion in his office behind the reception.

There is no way I can pretend that I wasn't doing my best to earwig on what was being said but, even walking slowly, once I'd reached the far side of the lobby, I had no further excuse to linger.

'You took your time,' said Aunt Jessica as I slipped on the chair, she'd kept for me. 'Everything okay?'

'Sorry about that. Had to wait ages for the lift and there was no way I was going to lug all that equipment up all those stairs to the fifth floor.' I dropped my voice and continued, 'Our Middle Eastern friend is making a hell of a fuss back there. He's having a good old set-to with the manager.'

Irene, who was sitting on the far side of Aunt Jessica leant forward and asked sotto voce, 'Are you talking about Yusef Kaya?'

'Is that his name?' My temperature rose a notch. It was one thing to tell Aunt Jessica but the last thing I wanted was to be seen as a gossip, tittle-tattling about other members of the party.

'What was it about? Do you know?' A deep frown furrowed Irene's forehead.

'As far as I could make out, he claims while we were all at the lecture, someone went into his room.'

'Has anything been taken?'

'I've no idea. I didn't stop to hear the details.'

To my relief, a waiter appeared at my elbow.

'This looks good,' I said politely as a plate of rice covered in a spicy stew was placed in front of me.

I asked the waiter what it was and was told it was a chicken dish. To be honest, despite my comment, I'm always a little wary of foreign food. Nonetheless, the rich aroma made me realise just how hungry I was. It had been a long time since my last decent meal.

We'd all been served and were busy tucking in before a morose-looking Yusef arrived.

As he passed behind her chair, Irene lent back and said, 'Harry says your room has been burgled. Have they taken much?'

She might be a lovely lady, but I could cheerfully have throttled Irene for dropping me in it like that.

Yusef glared then slowly shook his head. 'Nothing is missing but my things have been moved.'

'Are you sure it wasn't just one of the housekeeping staff dropping off extra towels and tidying up for you?' Irene suggested.

The only answer she received was another scowl before he marched to an empty seat at the far end of the table.

Conversation was a little stilted after that and to break the tension, I turned to the woman sitting next to me. 'I'm Harry. I'm Jessica's nephew.'

'Helen and Phil.' She indicated the man sitting next to her. He had a short grey beard with a full head of hair that was several shades darker.

He leant across his wife and shook my hand. 'I assume you've done this trip before?'

'No. This is my first time. Aunt Jessica's an old hand but this is all new to me. I gather from the question you asked about the golden age of Persian art that you're already familiar with the country and its history.'

'I wouldn't say that. I'm aware of many of the names that Jessica mentioned but I did a fair amount of reading before we came.'

His wife chuckled. 'He always does. For every holiday. Raids the local library and spends hours on the internet. Says it adds to his enjoyment of his holiday.'

'I think you get more out of what you're seeing when you see it in context,' he said defensively.

'Yes, dear.' Helen had obviously heard his justification many times before. She turned to me. 'That's what you have to put up with when you marry a teacher.'

'Is history your subject?' I asked him.

'Was. I retired last summer.'

'He was Deputy Head at Gravesend Grammar and now he's finding it hard adjusting to not having people to boss around anymore.'

'I didn't realise grammar schools were still in existence.'

It was Helen who answered. 'You'll find a lot in Kent.'

'Were you a teacher too?' I asked.

'I taught in a primary school, but I retired at sixty. We've wanted to visit Persia for years, but we could never travel in term time and, as the company only offers this trip in November, we had to wait until we'd both retired.'

I was still only halfway through my dessert when Aahil announced we'd be leaving in ten minutes. Like most of the others, Aunt Jessica had started her meal long before I arrived. She pushed away her empty plate and sat back.

'Don't wait for me. I'll be up in a sec.'

I shovelled in the last few mouthfuls and hurried out. I knew I wouldn't be the last as Yusef was still bending Aahil's ear at the far end of the table, but I didn't want to be accused of trying to listen in, especially after Irene's previous announcement.

After last time, rather than wait for the lift, I hurried along the corridor to the stairs. Off to my right were a series of window alcoves each with settees and small tables. In one of them, I spotted Mr Kamali talking with Irene. Their voices were low, and in any case, I was moving quickly, but it seemed to me that their conversation was quite heated. He appeared quite agitated. Irene had her back to me so I couldn't read her facial expression, but her body language was decidedly animated.

I told Aunt Jessica as we came back down a little later.

'I'm not sure what to make of it all, but I had the distinct impression that those two already know each other.'

'Are you sure? She may have noticed that he was upset about his encounter with Yusef and wanted to apologise for the rudeness of a fellow guest. She seems the mothering type to me. What makes you think they'd met before?'

'I can't quite put my finger on it, but the way they were talking together didn't seem like a manager/guest relationship somehow. It was as though he was not just upset but upset with her.'

'I think you might be letting your imagination run away with you. Just because of what happened last time, There's no need to start creating mysteries where they don't exist.'

CHAPTER 5

The Crown Jewels Museum was housed in a vault beneath the central branch of Tehran's national bank. We were not allowed to take photos, so most people, including me, bought a small but beautifully illustrated museum guide from the tiny shop near the entrance.

Yusef was clearly still angry about what he claimed had happened earlier. He stood to one side and made no attempt to look in the glass cases displaying souvenir mementoes and a selection of attractive postcards of the various items we were about to see. He spent most of his time glaring around the room at everyone else.

'There's more security here than at the airport. Even at the Tower of London we didn't have to go through all this palaver to see the British crown jewels,' I muttered to my aunt as I handed over my camera and phone.

'That's because this is the largest and most valuable collection of royal regalia anywhere in the world. It includes the world's largest pink diamond said to have decorated the crown of Cyrus the Great. Several of the Shahs commissioned their own jewel-encrusted crown and throne. Now known as the Treasury of National Jewels, it's state property and underpins the country's reserves backing all Iranian currency. Though its value is far more than its economic worth. It represents the artistic and cultural heritage of what was one of the grandest and richest empires the world has ever seen.'

We then had to line up to go through the electronic security screens. I must have looked the innocent, innocuous type but Yusef, who was immediately behind me was taken to one side for an extra grilling. He was made to stand arms out while a guard ran a wand over his torso and along each arm and leg. Then he had to empty his pockets, pulling out the lining to show they were empty. Not surprisingly, he protested vociferously.

'Couldn't have happened to a nicer fella.'

'Harry!'

It wasn't until I'd heard my aunt's sharp retort that I realised I'd said it out loud.

'Well,' I muttered defensively. 'You have to admit he's not exactly done much to make himself popular since he joined us. There's something distinctly odd about that man. Look at all that fuss he made in the hotel before lunch, and everywhere we go, he takes a quick look round to see who's following us.'

It took a while for our party to shuffle through. Gordon Hurley, a respectable-looking, balding man in his mid-to-late sixties, who no one could suspect as any kind of potential thief, was given the same treatment even if the search was far more perfunctory than that meted out to Yusef.

Even after we made our way down into the depths of the building we still had to wait in the queue before we were allowed into the vault itself.

As Aunt Jessica chatted to the couple behind us, I smiled at the woman in front.

'It's Harry, isn't it? I'm Paula. I think you and I must be the only ones on this trip who aren't drawing their pension.'

I'm no good at judging people's ages, but I put the tall, athletic-looking woman somewhere in her early forties. She was the chatty, outgoing type; easy to talk to, and I soon learnt that she worked in the offices of one of the national newspapers.

'Don't tell me you're an investigative journalist here on a major scoop? Are you hot on the trail of an international criminal who's using our holiday tour as cover? Let me guess. It has to be our mysterious Middle Eastern guy. I thought the authorities were about to nab him back there, but he must have hidden the evidence.'

'Idiot.' She gave me a playful punch. 'Sadly, I'm strictly a backroom research assistant. Mainly collating material for obituaries, though I am occasionally let out to do the odd theatre review. The highlight of my career so far has been a last-minute replacement for the guy supposed to cover a society wedding when half his office went down with 'flu last month. It was only a brief paragraph to go with a photo and hidden at the bottom of the society pages, but I did get up close and personal to a couple of minor royals plus a load of celebrities including the Beckhams.'

One of the officials came to remove the rope that held back the line.

'Let's hope we get a decent guide showing us round,' I said. 'My aunt warned me most of these guys are good but there are a few whose English leaves a lot to be desired.'

Sadly, we ended up with a stinker. Not that his English was particularly poor, although it was heavily accented, but he reeled off his script like a parrot at top speed and became impatient with anyone who tried to linger. I appreciated that it was his job to keep us all together, but I'd have sworn he missed out several display cabinets in his haste to rush us through. I listened in to some of the other guides around us and not only were they much more enthusiastic, but they also gave their groups far more detail about the various displays than our guy. Perhaps he was late for his tea-break.

It was only a short walk to the Glassware and Ceramic Museum, and everyone was so busy discussing the wonders they'd just seen, that it was not long before the group became strung out. As we made our way down a narrow path alongside one of the less busy side streets, Aahil waited at the corner for us all to catch up.

I was chatting with Gordon and Mary Hurley when someone's mobile started ringing. I knew from the ringtone it couldn't be mine. Gordon automatically began patting his pockets, but, just a few paces ahead of us, it was Yusef who pulled out his phone.

He had stopped so suddenly that Irene, following in his wake, almost bumped into him.

'I'm so sorry.'

Yusef ignored her. All his attention was on answering his caller. As people started to bunch up behind him, he stepped into the road without looking.

It all happened in an instant. I heard the roar of the engine as a car whizzed past me. Suddenly, it veered towards the kerb. Then as if in slow motion, Yusef's body was thrown up into the air. I heard rather than saw it hit the bonnet. Then it sailed over the windscreen and landed on the far side of the road right in the path of a small van coming the other way. I could see the horror in the wide eyes of the driver as he jammed his foot on the brake. Then came a resounding crunch as the van collided with the body.

CHAPTER 6

Stunned silence turned to noisy screaming. I was vaguely aware of people rushing towards the crumpled body, but I was too busy trying to stop myself from throwing up in the gutter. Eyes down, I turned away from the scene, stumbled to the wall and slumped down with my back against it, head between my knees.

My memory is a bit hazy after that. How long I stayed there, I've no idea. Probably no more than a minute. I felt a hand on my knee and realised Aunt Jessica was squatting beside me.

'You okay, sweetie?'

I nodded.

She helped me to my feet and gently steered me out of the general melee. Heaven knows where all these people had suddenly come from.

After the initial shock, I managed to pull myself together pretty quickly. Some of the others weren't so lucky and needed my help. Witnessing the horrific incident had brought on a bad attack of Mary's asthma and she was fighting for breath. Her Ventolin inhaler didn't seem to be having much effect. As my aunt attempted to calm her down, I tried to reassure her husband Gordon who was beside himself with worry, which wasn't helping Mary.

At that point, the police were on the scene. Their first concern was to clear the immediate area and it didn't make Mary's situation any easier especially when the young officer attempting to corral us all further down the street, started shouting at us in Farsi when the four of us failed to move on as instructed.

No doubt attracted by the commotion, a more senior officer arrived. He didn't speak English either, but he could at least appreciate the problem and sent someone to fetch help.

The younger officer came back with a smiling elderly man who said in stilted English, 'Come my shop. Sit inside.'

The shop was only a couple of doors away, but we made slow progress.

'I'll ring Aahil and let him know where we are,' said Aunt Jessica.

When she joined us again, she said, 'The police won't let anyone back into the street. They're keeping everyone well away from the scene of the accident.'

'What about the others?'

'They're all with Aahil. Everyone is still very upset as you might expect and wanted to know what's happened to the four of us. At the moment, everyone has to stay where they are until the police have taken statements from those who actually witnessed what happened.'

Ten minutes later, Mary's breathing was beginning to quieten, and she was no longer hunched forward pushing down on her fists in the attempt to get air into her lungs. Her face was drained of colour, and she looked utterly exhausted, but I was no longer worried about the urgency of finding a doctor.

'I'm so sorry.'

'No need to apologise,' I said. I'm no medic, but as I gave her wrist a reassuring squeeze, I could tell her pulse was still racing.

Gordon took her hand. 'It was probably the shock. She hasn't had a bad attack like this for years.'

Aunt Jessica's mobile rang. 'I see... No problem... I understand.'

It was impossible to make sense of what was being said

from her brief responses and we had to wait until the end of the call before she could explain.

'Will do… thanks, Aahil. See you soon.'

'Well?' I demanded, before she'd even had a chance to replace her phone in her pocket.

'It seems that the police have decided to let Aahil take the rest of the party back to the hotel and wait for an English-speaking officer to come and take witness statements from everyone. From what I could gather, right now, several of them are still too upset to be coherent in any case. To be honest, Aahil sounds barely coherent himself.'

'If the police are anything like the couple we encountered, I don't suppose any of them attending the scene speak English anyway.'

Aunt Jessica nodded then turned to Mary. 'How are you feeling now?'

Mary forced a smile, 'Much better.'

'I'll ring for a taxi.'

When we arrived back to the hotel, we discovered the rest of the group clustered in a corner of the cavernous lobby. They had only arrived a couple of minutes earlier and Aahil was still at the reception desk, presumably explaining what had happened.

'I don't suppose Mr Kamali is going to be overjoyed when he hears that the police are about to descend on the place. It won't do his hotel's reputation much good,' I said to Aunt Jessica.

'Indeed, it won't.'

At this time in the afternoon there were not many other people around, but I had grave doubts that either he or the police would want witness statements to be taken in such a public place.

Before I had a chance to voice my thoughts out loud, Mr Kamali appeared in person. He bustled over to the group with Aahil in tow several paces behind.

'My dear friends, please accept my sincere condolences for the loss of your friend and fellow passenger. Come, come everyone let me show you somewhere quiet where you may sit and recover after your upsetting experience.'

Talking nonstop, like some protective hen gently ushering her offspring to a place of safety, he guided us to a nearby lounge room. Like all the public rooms it was vast and opulent with a high ceiling and with enormous high-backed crimson velvet settees and deep enveloping armchairs arranged facing each other across an ornate low table.

As though for mutual protection, we all gravitated to one corner. Before we'd had a chance to take off our coats and find a seat, waiters appeared with trays of tea and small glasses of pale-yellow liquid which I assumed was some sort of local spirit provided for foreign tourists. Then plates of food arrived, mostly small, sweet delicacies, and were laid out on the table.

'Eat, eat,' Mr Kamali urged. 'Sugar is good for shock.'

I helped pull one of the heavy armchairs into the circle for Paula to sit down and went to perch on the wide arm of the long settee alongside it, next to Aunt Jessica.

'Room for a little one here,' Aunt Jessica said as she moved to make more space.

'Mary seems to have recovered,' I said, once I'd settled myself next to her.

'Yes, thank goodness. I think now she's more embarrassed at having caused a fuss than anything else.'

I stifled a yawn. 'Now I'm sat down, I don't know if it's because my sleep patterns are up the creek after the change of time zones or the after-effects of what's just happened, but I suddenly feel dead on my feet. I hope we don't have to wait long for these policemen to arrive; I could do with a quick kip.'

As if on cue, the door opened again. All eyes turned to look at the three men being shown in by Mr. Kamali. Even though they were not in uniform, their whole manner exuded authority. What he lacked in stature, the older man made up for with his upright carriage and military bearing as he strode towards us.

'Ladies and gentlemen, I am Inspector Tabar. I will not keep you for longer than necessary. I have spoken to your guide, and I understand you were all with Mr Yusef Kaya when the accident occurred.' He turned and indicated Aahil who was still hovering by the door. 'It would be helpful if any of you can tell me about the car that hit Mr Kaya.'

No one was able to identify the make or model or even agree on the exact colour though the general consensus was that it was dark, that the driver had not slowed but raced away.

'I understand that Mr Kaya was walking at the rear of the group. Did any of you witness the actual impact?'

I raised my hand and for one awful moment I thought that I was going to be the only one but gradually a few others reluctantly joined me.

'He just stepped off the pavement. Right into the path of that car.' Mary shuddered at the memory and put her hands to her face as though the action could blot out that awful picture.

'That's right,' blurted out her husband. 'It all happened so quickly.'

The inspector raised a hand to stop the murmurs that broke out. 'Please ladies and gentlemen! We need to speak to each of you individually. My men will be round to take statements from you all, but I would like to start with those who raised their hands. If the rest of you would please be patient, we will speak to you as soon as possible.'

I had the privilege, if you can call it that, of speaking to the Inspector himself. Not that he kept me for long. He asked a few questions and wanted to know why I'd become separated from the rest of the party when the area was cleared after the accident. He took my name and made a few notes but that was it.

The moment the police left, waiters appeared again with fresh tea and copious plates of particularly appetising-looking small snacks and sandwiches. Apart from Mary and Gordon who decided to go straight up to their room, everyone began to tuck in.

'No idea what was in it, but it was very tasty,' I admitted as I polished off my third pastry. 'I hadn't realised how hungry I was.'

'Does anyone know what we're supposed to do next?' asked Paula. 'It's obviously too late to go to the museum now, but what are we doing about dinner? Are we stopping here or going out to a restaurant?'

'Not a clue,' I replied. 'Let's ask Aahil. Has anyone seen him?'

'I think he went with the Inspector when they left,' someone volunteered.

'More likely in some corner trying to pull himself together.' It was said sotto voce, but even though Paula was staring at the glass of tea she was clutching in her lap, I knew the comment was intended for me to hear.

'Meaning?' I said just as softly.

'Poor lad went to pieces out there when the accident happened. Just stood there staring. If it hadn't been for Phil calming everyone down and organising things, we might still all be out there. It was left to him to phone Hassan to come and collect us.'

Even if Paula hadn't mentioned him by name, I'd have guessed if anyone was needed to take charge of the group, it would have been Phil who stepped up. There was an air of authority about the bearded ex-teacher I'd spoken to at lunch.

I turned to Aunt Jessica, 'I'm just going to see if I can find out where Aahil's got to.'

She shook her head, but before she could tell me not to, I jumped up and hurried to the door.

I made my way to the reception area. There was no sign

of Aahil, but I did spot Irene talking with the manager again. I was about to go and ask if either of them had seen him, when Mr Kamili suddenly shook his head. His normal smiling face broke into an anxious frown, and he began talking quickly. I had no idea what had upset him, but Irene put a hand on his shoulder, and he appeared to calm down.

I had no choice but to quickly backtrack and hope neither of them had spotted me.

CHAPTER 7

'Couldn't find Aahil anywhere,' I announced when I arrived back. Not that there were many of the party left in the room to tell.

Aunt Jessica gave an exasperated sigh. 'I expect he's gone back home now the police have left. You rushed off like a mad thing before I had a chance to say anything.'

'But what about tonight?'

'As I told the others after you disappeared, dinner is in the hotel this evening. Everyone is free to eat at whatever time they like. The formal restaurant upstairs opens at eight-thirty or, for those who'd fancy something lighter, they can choose something from the buffet in the Garden Room anytime from six o'clock onwards. A few of us have decided to meet up in there at seven. So, if you're ready, Harry, shall we go up to our rooms?'

I collected up our stuff and followed her out to the lifts.

'You made me feel like a right idiot, just now. Telling me off like that in front of everyone.' If I was honest, most of the party had already left the room but I still felt aggrieved at being spoken to like some naughty schoolboy.

Ignoring my comment, she said, 'What on earth made you go charging off like that?'

'I was worried about Aahil, that's all.'

'You really should be more circumspect. You're making your interest in our attractive young guide a little too obvious.'

'We were only chatting earlier.' I tried to sound blasé.

'And when it comes down to it, it's only natural we should gravitate to each other. All the rest of the men in the party are at least thirty years older.'

'Maybe, but you need to keep a bit more distance. Just remember where you are.'

'Paula said he was badly shaken by the accident, and she wasn't sure he was coping. Didn't you see how nervous he was when he came in with the detectives? He must be really worried about his job. I mean, he is supposed to be responsible for our safety. He could get into a lot of trouble.'

The look she gave me indicated my glib comment had not deceived her.

In the end, apart from Mary and Gordon, everyone turned up at the Garden Room.

'I'm not sure I'm really all that hungry,' admitted Barbara. Even she seemed subdued for once. 'I thought I'd come and be sociable.'

'You can just have soup,' suggested Aunt Jessica. 'Or there's a salad bar where you can choose whatever takes your fancy. I think I might join you. Shall we go and see?'

The man sitting opposite me wrinkled his nose, pushed back his chair and said, 'Well, I for one am not a great lover of rabbit food. I'm off to see what's in those silver dishes on the hot food table.'

'Good idea,' I said and followed the tall guy with a definite American twang in his accent.

'I'm sorry, I've forgotten your name,' I said as I peeled back the lid of one of the tureens.

'I'm Robert and my wife's Caroline. You're Jessica's nephew, Harry, right?'

'For my sins. What have you got there?' I asked peering into tureen he had opened.

'The label says Ghormeh Sabzi. It's some sort of stew but what exactly is in it, I'm none the wiser. Oh well, I'll give it a whirl.' He ladled a generous spoonful onto his plate and opened the next container.

I decided to be a great deal more circumspect and eventually helped myself to two long skewers with cubes of chicken and slices of roasted vegetables.

'There's quite an assortment of things to choose from,' I said when I returned to the table.

As if by some unspoken mutual consent, no one referred to the accident and it was only towards the end of the meal that Barbara asked about the arrangements for the next day that Yusef's name came up.

'I presume we'll carry on with the itinerary as planned,' she said. 'I don't see why the police would want to speak to us again. I wonder what will happen to his things.'

'I presume one of the staff will pack them up and send them back to his family,' said Aunt Jessica.

'Does anyone know where he lived?' asked Caroline. Unlike her husband, she had no discernible American accent. 'I never had the chance to speak to him, did anyone else?'

'I did,' said Barbara. 'Only very briefly. I sat next to him at lunch, but he wasn't much of a talker. I just said how much I was looking forward to seeing Persepolis and I asked if he'd ever been there. He said no. It was his first time in Iran. He was brought up in Turkey but moved to London a few years ago to join his brother in the family business.

'There's a big Middle Eastern community in West London in the area I live. Mostly shop keepers. Their stores are really popular. Good quality and very reasonable prices and open almost twenty-four hours a day. A few doors down from my flat is this fantastic little corner shop. The family who run it are really popular in the community, not just with the Persians and the Iraqis, but everyone in the area. I'm in there all the time. Outside on the pavement are fruit and vegetable stalls and inside is like an Aladdin's cave of all sorts of things Persian. That's what made me so keen to come on this trip. The people are so friendly and welcoming. Always smiling and happy to see you. It's taken me years to save up but coming here has been on my bucket list for decades.'

Barbara's enthusiasm wasn't shared by everyone.

'Maybe, but you can hardly claim Yusef was exactly the friendly type. I know you shouldn't speak ill of the dead, but I never saw that man smile. More interested in talking to someone on his phone rather than to any of us,' said Robert.

'That's true,' agreed Paula. 'If he hadn't stepped off the pavement into the path of that car to answer that call, the accident would never have happened.'

'Shall we talk about something a bit less gloomy?' Irene interrupted. 'I'm really looking forward to seeing Golestan Palace tomorrow. I Googled it back home a few days ago and the pictures looked amazing. There's this glittering reception room with an enormous gold throne. It's so huge it swallows the model sitting on it which is supposed to be life-size.'

'I saw that too. There's another throne as well. It's twice the size if not more. The marble platform is held up by all these marble figures.'

It was almost nine o'clock when the party broke up.

'You're very quiet,' Aunt Jessica remarked as we walked along the corridor to our rooms. 'Feeling tired?'

'Not really. I was just thinking about something Mary said when the Inspector came to interview us.'

'Oh?'

'About Yusef stepping into the path of that car.'

'What about it?'

I shrugged my shoulders. 'It's probably nothing, but I could have sworn… I probably imagined it.'

She opened her door, pushed it open and waved me in.

'I thought you said you were ready for an early night what with the jetlag and all the day's excitement,' I protested.

'Never mind that now.' She gently pushed me inside then closed the door. 'What's troubling you?'

'I know it sounds fanciful, but I could have sworn that car accelerated then deliberately swerved to hit him.'

'You didn't mention it to the Inspector.'

'No. There wasn't much time to think about it after it happened what with seeing to Mary. When I thought about it afterwards, it didn't seem to make much sense.'

'Why on earth would anyone want to kill Yusef?'

She had a point. 'I know it doesn't make sense. Apart from anything else, how did the driver know what street Yusef would be in at that precise time, let alone that he would step off the pavement at that exact moment?'

'Precisely.'

I sank down on the bed, and after a brief moment looked up at her. 'Nonetheless, I can't shake off the feeling that Yusef's death was no accident. That the opportunity suddenly arose, and the driver went for him.'

'Would you be so convinced if someone else had been killed and not Yusef?'

'What do you mean?'

'Let's face it, you've been obsessed with the man from the start of the holiday. On the way from the airport, you marked him out as a suspicious character simply on the basis he made a phone call.'

'That's ridiculous.'

'You have to admit, the man does seem to have got under your skin.'

'I can't say I took to him, that's true, but there's no way you can convince me that that driver didn't have Yusef in his sights when he drove straight at him. And whatever I may have thought about him, no one deserves to die like that.'

Silence hung in the air. Eventually, she said, 'In which case, I think we need to find out a bit more about our strange fellow-passenger.'

CHAPTER 8

We were down to breakfast early next morning. Not that we had the place to ourselves, but all the other guests dotted around the room appeared to be Iranian.

'Have you noticed how many of them have plasters across their noses? I noticed several in here last evening when we were having dinner.'

Aunt Jessica poured herself another cup of tea and said, 'They're here for nose jobs.'

'I beg your pardon!'

'A great many Iranians have very prominent Roman noses, so they come to Tehran for plastic surgery to remove the bump.'

'But there are men as well as women.'

'You think men aren't just as vain?'

'I thought they were all supposed to be beautiful.'

'The majority are. That's the problem. If you had a single blemish that stopped you from being stunning, wouldn't you want to get rid of it if you could afford it?'

'I suppose so.'

We finished our meal but as we walked towards the lifts, Aunt Jessica, suddenly stopped.

'Something wrong?'

'Not at all. I've just thought of something. You go on up, I'll see you later.'

She'd gone before I had a chance to ask what she was up to.

I knocked and the door opened a crack and Aunt Jessica peered round it.

'Are you ready to go down?'

'Aah, it's you. Come in.'

'Who were you expecting?'

'I didn't realise it was quite so late and I thought it might be someone from reception and I haven't put my scarf on yet. I keep forgetting when we're in the hotel.'

She bustled around and it was a couple of minutes before she collected all the stuff she needed for the day.

'Take that for me, would you, sweetie.' She handed me her tote bag and went to the mirror to arrange her scarf.

'I think that's everything.'

'Don't forget your camera.'

'Thanks. Okay, let's go.'

As we walked towards the lift, I couldn't hold back my curiosity any longer. 'What was so urgent that you rushed off after breakfast? I checked your room ten minutes ago and you still hadn't come back up.'

'I went to find Mr Kamali and it took some time to find him.'

The lift doors opened and there were several other guests already inside. As we squeezed in to join them, Aunt Jessica said, 'Tell you about it later.'

Aahil was already waiting when we reached the reception area. He was looking considerably more relaxed than the last time I'd seen him. He and Aunt Jessica went into a huddle to check on the day's arrangements, so I went to sit on one of the settees to wait for the others to arrive.

The first to put in an appearance was Paula. She looked very elegant in the silky long tailored jacket that, rather than concealing her shapely figure, actually enhanced it. She must have spent some time artfully arranging the soft folds of the scarf that framed her face and nestled around her shoulders.

'I don't know about the Archaeology Museum; you look ready for the film set.'

'Thank you, kind sir. Do you like it?' She put out her arms and gave me a twirl. 'The jacket cost a bomb. My wardrobe didn't contain many tops that conformed to Iran's ridiculous dress code for women, so I had to do a fair amount of shopping. I didn't intend to spend so much but once I saw it, I had to have it.'

'That jewelled emerald pattern certainly brings out the colour in your eyes.'

She giggled. 'My eyes are *not* green.'

She sank down beside me, stretched out her long legs in front of her and stared across at Aahil and my aunt. 'Well, our dishy guide looks a lot happier this morning, I must say.'

'Down lady, down. He's far too young for you.'

In a sudden about turn of mood, she said, 'Has there been any news about the police catching the hit-and-run driver?'

'Not that I've heard.'

'I don't suppose we'll ever know unless they're caught before we leave Tehran tomorrow morning.'

She waited for my answer, but I just shrugged.

'Odd don't you think, going that fast in the middle of the city? The driver must have been going at quite a lick to throw the body up into the air like that.'

'I'd rather not think about it.'

Completely ignoring my comment, she mused, 'They could have been joyriders, I suppose. Which probably means they abandoned the car straight away.'

'Do they get joy-riders in Iran?'

'Heaven knows. Perhaps the driver already had points on his licence and couldn't afford to lose it.'

Much to my relief, some of the others were now arriving and the subject was dropped.

'The National Museum houses Persian artefacts from all the ancient sites, but I'd like to start our visit by showing you this map.'

Aahil led us into the first gallery. We gathered round as he began with a brief description of the physical geography of the country that ranged from rugged mountain chains surrounding high interior basins. He explained the effect the terrain had on the history of the occupation of this vast area that even today is seven times larger than the UK.

Aahil was in his element. There could be no doubt about his passion and pride in his country's rich history and it was difficult to equate the enthusiastic articulate guide with the timid, helpless young man I'd last seen the day before.

Every now and then as we toured the various galleries, Aunt Jessica would point out some details on one of the exhibits and elaborate on its history.

'If you look at this rather magnificent bronze statue, you can see his long moustache and distinctive headgear typical of a Parthian nobleman. The Parthians were famous horsemen. Their military strength lay in their mounted archers who were just as deadly when they turned in the saddle and fired their arrows behind them as they retreated.'

'Just when you think the danger's past, it turns to bite you.'

I'd said it as a joke, but yesterday's hit-and-run must have been playing on my mind because my choice of words suddenly made me picture the car, like some Parthian horseman charging at Yusef. But what made me go cold was the feeling that the trouble wasn't over and there was more to come.

Putting such bizarre thoughts behind me, I tried to concentrate on what Aunt Jessica was telling us. After over an hour, my head was reeling with the overload of information about Medes, Seleucids, Seljuks, Safavids and Qajars and I was beginning to glaze over. My concentration had gone to pot.

I still hadn't been able to pump Aunt Jessica about her

mysterious mission after breakfast. I waited until she'd finished answering yet another of Barbara's questions then took her by the elbow and gently steered her to one side where we couldn't be overheard.

'It's driving me mad wondering why all the secrecy about what you were up to this morning. If you don't tell me here and now, I'll lose my temper.'

She gave me a beaming smile. 'I wanted to have a word with Mr Kamali – find out more about why Yusef insisted someone had been in his room, especially if nothing was taken. I went to reception, but he wasn't there. I could hardly ask the woman behind the desk without looking like a nosey busybody…'

'Which you are, of course.'

'Do you want to hear what happened or not?'

I grinned.

'I told them that the tour company had asked me to pack up all his things and arrange for them to be sent back to the Britain.'

'Did they?'

'Of course not! Anyway, the reason that it all took so long is the girl on the desk had to send for Mr Kamali. When he eventually turned up, he insisted there was no need for me to trouble myself with it and he would see that one of his staff would deal with it. You know how helpful he likes to be. It took all my powers of persuasion to convince him to let me do it.'

'Did you get to ask him what happened about Yusef's complaint?'

'Oh yes. Once we'd finished, I mentioned I thought it strange Yusef was so certain someone had been in his room if nothing was taken. If robbery wasn't the motive, what possible reason could anyone have for going in? According to Mr Kamali, Yusef admitted that, though there was no evidence to prove there'd been an intruder, he gave him no more explanation than he gave us. Just insisted someone had been in his room and searched his belongings.'

'Is it possible that something was taken but Yusef dare not tell anyone what it was? Something he shouldn't have had in the first place?'

'I see what you're getting at but if that were the case, he'd have kept it on him.'

'Perhaps he'd deliberately laid a trap to check no one had been in his room while he was gone.'

Aunt Jessica shook her head. 'Don't get carried away. You've been watching too many spy films.'

'Probably. But I get this feeling he was worried that he was being followed. Why else did he keep looking over his shoulder all the time?'

'To get back to reality, when we return to the hotel this evening, I have permission to collect a room key from reception and you and I can have a good nose around his things and see what we can find out about our mysterious Mr Yusef Kaya and why he joined this tour. It certainly wasn't because he fancied a holiday.'

CHAPTER 9

Once we were back on the coach, Aahil announced that it was time for lunch.

'The choice is yours, ladies and gentlemen. Hassan can drive us to one of the restaurants or would you prefer a light lunch? Bearing in mind, we are booked into the main restaurant for a set meal this evening, how hungry is everyone?'

'A coffee and a sandwich would do me,' said Gordon.

'I couldn't face a big meal either,' agreed Barbara.

'Everyone happy with that?' There were no dissenters. 'In which case, I know an excellent little coffee shop that bakes its own really good cakes. It's very popular with the locals.'

'What do you fancy to drink?' asked Aunt Jessica as she studied the menu card in the centre of the small metal table.

'A straightforward white coffee will suit me fine,' I replied, still busy arranging my camera gear on the spare chair.

There was only one waiter, and it took a few minutes for him to come and take our order.

'What sort of cakes do you have?' I asked him.

'They are on display on the counter if you would like go over and choose.'

It was a difficult decision. In the end, Aunt Jessica and I decided to go shares on a slice of honey cake and one crumbly nutty variety.

When we went back to our places, Irene was still sitting at the next table waiting for the other occupants to return.

'You not having a cake?'

She shook her head. 'I'm waiting for my hot chocolate. I think that's it coming now.'

The waiter put a tall sundae glass topped with a mound of whipped cream in front of her and we chatted across the gap until Barbara and Paula returned.

The tables were so close together, it was impossible not to catch odd snatches of conversation from the next table. From what she was saying, I gathered that Barbara lived in an area of London with a sizable Iranian community. When Paula asked if she knew why so many Iranians had made their homes in London, my ears pricked up.

'It's very noticeable that neither the Iranians nor the Iraqis will talk about it; especially those who came over in the late 1970s and '80s. If ever you start asking, they have this way of turning the conversation back to you. You quickly learn it's a taboo subject.'

'Could it be anything to do with the Shah's secret police, do you think?'

'Probably more to do with the Iran-Iraq war.'

Irene suddenly cut into the conversation. 'I'm looking forward to seeing the Golestan Palace this afternoon.'

I had the distinct impression she wanted them to drop the subject altogether, but her attempts proved unsuccessful. Paula was nothing if not persistent. She carried on as though Irene hadn't spoken.

'My dad was in that part of the world at the time. He claimed people in Britain didn't appreciate just how bitter that Gulf War was. It wasn't only soldiers who died. There were just as many civilians killed. Over a million of them. He was very scathing about the CIA. According to him, that war would never have gone on for eight years if they hadn't…'

A chair scraped as a couple of local businessmen sat down at the table on our other side and I couldn't catch the rest of Paula's comment. Over the top of my coffee, I looked across at Aunt Jessica. Though she also had her nose buried in her cup, it was evident that she'd been listening to the conversation across the way as closely as I had been.

One of the new arrivals lifted his briefcase onto the table, snapped open the catches and spread several large sheets of paper in front of the other who took out a pen. They began loudly discussing the contents, thus drowning out any chance of hearing what our fellow passengers were saying.

When Paula and the others went to pay their bills, I looked at Aunt Jessica and said, 'Am I imagining it, or is our reporter sniffing for a story do you think?'

Aunt Jessica raised an eyebrow. 'She's certainly done her homework.'

There was no time to discuss it further as we had to join the rest of the party.

Golestan Palace was everything and more than we'd been promised. It had to be the greatest collection of vast spectacular halls ever seen. In the famous Hall of Mirrors, light from the line of crystal chandeliers hanging from the ceiling was reflected not only in the great mirrors that lined its walls but also the thousands of tiny pieces of mosaic that formed the frames and the coving and the ceiling above.

'The mirrors came from Venice, but many arrived broken after the long sea journey. Nonetheless, as you can see, the craftsmen wasted nothing which explains the vast numbers of mirror mosaics throughout the palace. You can even see the in the corridors,' Aahil explained.

When we reach the reception hall, I stood just inside the entrance trying to take it all in.

'Louis XIV, see this and weep!' I said to no one in particular. 'If he could have seen this, he'd have torn down Versailles and started again.'

There was a girlish giggle from behind me. 'I think I agree with you.'

I turned and smiled at Paula.

The palace provided an excellent background for our first group photo, with Aunt Jessica and Aahil kneeling at the front and the others gathered standing above.

'Difficult to tell but I think I managed at least a couple of decent shots,' I said to Aunt Jessica as we began to move on to another section of the palace. 'I'll have to wait until we get back and I can put them on the laptop. The trouble with group shots is that usually at least one person has their eyes closed. Still, I can always play around with the imaging software when I get home.'

'You're pleased with your latest investment then?'

'The camera gear? Oh yes though I'll be even happier when I've paid off the loan to buy it.' I'd only had it a month and I still winced at thought of how much it had all cost. But if I wanted to extend my business to include the promotional material, the extra lens and filters were essential to capture the shots I'd need for brochures, flyers and social media.

'At least you can put it all down as a tax expense.'

'That's true.'

We returned to the hotel well before five o'clock.

'As you all know, tomorrow morning we'll be taking an early flight to Kerman in the southwest. To save time having to check in and collect your cases when we arrive, Hassan will take them in the coach. As he will have to drive through the night to meet us at the airport, please would you each sort out what you need for this evening and bring your main cases down to the lobby straightaway. Hassan will be back to collect them in half an hour.'

'But he's been working all day,' protested Mary. 'When is the poor man going to get any sleep?'

'His co-driver will take over and they will take it in

turns.'

The coach drew up outside as Aunt Jessica and I came down.

Ali, the co-driver, was much younger than Hassan, only a few years older than me, with dark wavy hair and hooded eyes. He didn't have Hassan's ready smile and he didn't even look me in the face when I handed him my grip. Perhaps he was just shy.

Aunt Jessica and I didn't hang around. She was due to give a second talk before dinner so there wasn't much time for us to go through Yusef's things. She collected the key card for his room, and we made our way upstairs.

Either he wasn't the tidiest of people or the police had already searched his room. Most of his belongings were still in his case which lay open on the rack next to the wardrobe.

'Nothing in the drawers,' I said as Aunt Jessica sorted through the contents of his case.

'I'll fetch his wash things from the bathroom. And I suppose you'd better check he hasn't left shoes under the bed.'

I knelt down to look, and as I went to stand up again, I noticed something tucked right at back of the small cubbyhole beneath the bedside table. It wasn't easy to reach but after getting my arm at the right angle I was able to pull out the folded sheets of paper.

'It's the itinerary details sent by the tour company plus a couple of handout sheets from your first lecture wrapped round his passport.'

'I'm surprised the police didn't take that,' she said.

'I don't suppose they found it. I wouldn't have done if I hadn't been down on my knees and looking in that direction. It's a red passport so he must have had British nationality.' I looked inside to check. 'It's new. He only took it our three months ago. Not a good photo, but then they never are, are they?'

Aunt Jessica picked up the itinerary booklet and began flicking through the pages.

'Born 18th June 1956 in Izmir, Turkey.'

She looked up. 'Who does he give as his emergency contacts?'

I flicked to the back. 'He hasn't filled it in.'

'Oh well, the company will have it. It's on the booking form.'

As I handed everything over to her, I asked, 'Do you think it's genuine?'

'What on earth do you mean?'

I shook my head. 'I'm not suggesting it's a forgery, but I'm not convinced Yusef was Turkish. When he blew his top at the security gate, I'll swear he was swearing in Farsi.'

She put her hands on her hips, but before she could say anything, I continued quickly, 'I know what you're going to say. How on earth would I of all people know? But I'm certain he and the guard were speaking the same language.'

'Even if they were, the two countries share a border and there's no reason to suppose they hadn't learnt enough of each other's language for a basic exchange.'

As always, she had a point, but I wasn't ready to concede and muttered, 'But why would he learn the language when he claimed he'd never been to Iran?'

She shrugged and turned back to the booklet. 'For some reason he's circled Day 12.'

'Where are we then?'

'In Isfahan. But that's it – no notes to explain what's supposed to be happening on that day.'

'Anything else?'

'There's a few scribbled notes right at the back. But they're all in Arabic script. Probably not important, but I think I'll keep the booklet anyway. Whoever eventually gets his things won't want it. I suppose, we'd better send the passport back with everything else.

I closed the case and we both stood up. 'Shall I take this down to reception and you can go and get ready for your talk?'

'No don't bother. Leave it on the bed. Mr Kamali said one of his staff would collect it.'

CHAPTER 10

It was a big surprise when Aahil snuck in a few minutes after Aunt Jessica had started her lecture. After I'd set up the projector, I'd stayed at the back, otherwise I probably wouldn't have noticed him until the talk was over. I beckoned him to come and join us, but he shook his head and slid onto chair just inside the door. I turned back to look at the screen.

'Here you see the first of the Qajar rulers, Agha Mohammad who has the distinction of being the most brutal and hated of all the Iranian monarchs, which is saying something, believe you me. Very few of them were angels and a great many thought little of having brothers, uncles, even fathers, disposed of in their quest for power. He was a eunuch, castrated by his captors when he was a young man in an attempt to stop him trying to seize the throne.'

'Ouch! Enough to drive any guy into taking things out on all and sundry.' Robert's remark and the mock pain in his voice as he said it, resulted in laughter and a few more ribald comments concerning crown jewels.

When the laughter died down, she continued, 'But for all that, he succeeded and despite his vengeful nature, he united the country and managed to keep Persia intact after a period of considerable upheaval and infighting.'

It was a good opportunity for me to leave my seat discreetly and join Aahil.

'I thought you'd gone home,' I whispered.

He shook his head. 'I'm staying here tonight. Our lift to the airport will be here at six o'clock tomorrow morning and I live on the other side of the city.'

There was no time for the two of us to chat further at the end of the talk as it was my job to see to packing up the equipment and returning it upstairs.

'I can manage this lot on my own if you want to go and join the others,' I said to Aunt Jessica as I coiled the various leads and put them in the bag.

'No, I'll bring the laptop and you can take the rest.'

Once we'd put the stuff on the table in her room, I turned and said, 'Okay, so what is you want to tell me you don't want anyone else to hear.'

She smiled. 'You know me too well. It's just a thought that came to me when I saw Aahil slipping his phone into his pocket when he came into the lecture. One thing we didn't find when we searched Yusef's room was his mobile.'

'Of course not. Yusef had it with him. We know he was using it when he was hit.'

'True, but according to Mr Kamali, the police returned the rest of his things. So, what happened to it?'

'I expect it flew out of his hand with the impact.'

'Perhaps the police kept it as evidence. To discover who he was talking to at the time. Though perhaps they never did find it. With all the commotion going on, it could easily have been kicked somewhere and gone unnoticed. Or even picked up by someone?'

'Now who's being fanciful?'

'The more I think about it, I'm sure it holds the answer to the whole mystery.' She frowned in concentration. 'Who was he phoning when we left the airport? Was it the same person who rang him just before the accident? And what about his emails? They might reveal all sorts of things, like why he was here in Iran in the first place because, as I said before, I'll lay odds it wasn't because he fancied a holiday.'

When we eventually reached the restaurant, we found the rest of our party all sitting at one long table at the side of the room.

The meal began with soup. I peered suspiciously into the bowl of thick somewhat bilious-green liquid and asked the waiter what was in it. I couldn't understand his reply.

'What did he call it?' asked Barbara who was sitting opposite.

'Ashresh something or other.' I stirred the thick liquid.

'For goodness' sake, sweetie. Just try it.'

'It's quite tasty,' said Barbara encouragingly. 'Mainly noodles I think, with lots of spices I can't identify.'

Despite my misgivings, it was quite acceptable, and I had no problem emptying the bowl.

For our main course, four or five different dishes were laid out in the centre of the table for us to help ourselves. Aahil came down and told us about each one. Most people decided to try a little from each plate, going back for more of the ones they liked best.

Dinner broke up relatively early as everyone decided on an early night given that we were all due for a wakeup call at some ungodly hour.

'Will there be time for any breakfast before we leave the hotel?' asked Robert. He was a big man and obviously enjoyed his food.

'Coffee and cake will be available in the lobby a quarter of an hour before we leave. I do need everyone down there by five to six. We need to leave on time. We can't afford to get caught up in the early morning traffic or we will miss our flight,' Aahil reminded us all.

'Is it going to be any warmer in Kerman? It's a lot further south,' I asked Aunt Jessica when we returned to her room. 'My hands were quite chilly this afternoon when we were outside.'

'Nowhere is warm in Iran in November,' Aunt Jessica

replied distractedly as she inspected her scarf. 'It's surprisingly difficult to eat with this on. If you're not careful, the end slips off your shoulder as you lean forward over your plate and ends up in whatever you're trying to eat.'

'I could have sworn I read somewhere it was in the middle of a desert and can get up to thirty-odd degrees in the summer.'

'True but this is not summer and besides, Kerman might be on a desert plain but nonetheless, it's well over five-and-a-half thousand feet above sea level.' She was still inspecting the ends of her scarf for any food stains.

'Do you want me to take charge of the laptop and projector tomorrow?'

'Please. I can manage my camera. I only have my pyjamas and wash kit in my overnight bag. I changed before we went down this evening, so I'm going to wear the same clothes tomorrow. Would you like me to put your stuff in the same bag in the morning and then you'll only have the equipment to worry about when we get on the plane?'

'That would be great. Thanks.'

'Did you know the word pyjamas comes from the Persian word "paejamah" used for loose trousers that tie round the waist?'

'You learn something new every day.'

She threw me her disapproving schoolmistress look and said, 'I hope that's not all you've learnt today.'

I laughed. 'No. Though it would be nice to have learnt a bit more about our mysterious Yusef Kaya and why he booked on this tour. I'm still convinced he was Iranian and not a Turk at all. Why else would he have a brand-new passport and not bother to fill in that back page?'

'Suspicious, I agree. But there's no way to prove it.'

'That's not all.'

'Oh?'

'I know you'll say, I'm fantasising, but I'm convinced

Irene and Mr Kamali have met before.'

'I wouldn't be totally surprised myself. I saw the pair of them together again when I took Yusef's key back to reception.'

'You didn't tell me.'

'Don't sound so indignant. There wasn't time and I'd forgotten all about it until now. Why are you making such a big thing of it, anyway?'

'She gives every impression of being a sweet old lady but if she's so innocent why didn't she put her hand up when that inspector came to the hotel and asked who saw the car hit Yusef? She was immediately behind him just before he stepped into the road. She had to have seen exactly what happened because she was just a couple of feet away.'

'What are you suggesting? That she and Mr Kamali somehow conspired to kill Yusef? That's a flight of fancy even for your over-active imagination.'

'Of course not! I just think it's odd.'

She yawned. 'Anyway. We can't do anything about it right now, so let's get to bed.'

CHAPTER 11

By the time we had checked in and made our way to find a seat in the departure lounge, there was only half an hour before we were due to be called for boarding.

I was still trying to divest myself of all my equipment when Aunt Jessica said, 'Do you fancy another coffee before we board?'

'Please, and I wouldn't mind something to eat if they have anything. Something savoury if possible. I don't suppose we'll get any breakfast on the plane.'

'I'll see what there is.'

Once I'd settled myself, I turned to smile at Caroline in the seat next to me.

'I'm not sure I'm awake yet,' I said.

'Me neither. My body clock doesn't know what time it is. It's alright for Robert. He spent his whole working life jetting off all over the world, but I've never been further than the Canaries.'

'You never went with him then?'

'We've only been married three years. We didn't meet till Robert came to Britain after he retired.'

'You mean he's never taken you to the US to see his old home?'

She shook her head. 'He has no close family left over there and decided to make a clean break and settle down over here.'

'So how did the pair of you meet?'

She hesitated. 'Actually, we met online. A dating site for

older people.' She was obviously embarrassed about admitting to resorting to such unromantic methods.

'Good for you. These days it's so much more difficult to meet people socially, don't you think?' It was obviously the right thing to say because she looked relieved.

'I lost my first husband eight years ago and Robert had always been so busy travelling there'd never been time to settle down.'

'What did he do?'

'He was a business consultant and spent most of his time working abroad, mostly in the Middle East. To be honest, he never talks about it. What about you? I presume you don't spend all your time travelling with your aunt.'

We chatted on until Aunt Jessica returned.

It was only a short flight. I'd been allocated a window seat and I had my first taste of the vast barren, water-less plain bounded by distant mountains as the plane came into land. At first, I couldn't see a single building. My forward view was blocked by the wing, and when the wheels hit the ground, I had visions of us landing in the middle of nowhere far from any sign of human habitation.

As promised, the coach was waiting when we came out of the airport building. Hassan, looking none the worse for his night-time journey, welcomed us with his customary cheery smile as we all climbed onboard.

Despite my earlier misgivings, it was a relatively short journey to our hotel. The city obviously lay on the opposite side of the plane to where my aunt and I had been sitting. We were sent straight into breakfast while Aahil dealt with all the check-in details.

'I suppose this is technically brunch,' laughed Paula as we stood side by side at the buffet table, loading our plates from the large selection on offer.

'It all looks very tempting,' I agreed. 'I certainly won't want anything else until dinner tonight.'

She came to sit at our table.

'Our driver seems a friendly soul, but I'm not so sure about his assistant. He barely gave me a nod of acknowledgement when I spoke to him at the airport,' she said as she twirled the strands of some spiced vegetable around her fork and lifted it to her mouth.

'Perhaps he doesn't speak much English,' I replied.

'Hassan has a very basic grasp of the language. I don't know about Ali. I've never met him before. But I suspect both of them can understand a great deal more than they're able to say,' said Aunt Jessica.

I tucked into my meal and let the two women continue with their small talk.

'You've done this trip before I take it?'

Aunt Jessica nodded. 'The company only run this particular trip once a year, but I've done it for the last couple of years.'

'I was reading up on Kerman on the plane. I hadn't realised it was quite that old – dates back to the third century according to my guidebook. Built on the trade route between Persia and India.'

'Uh-huh,' agreed Aunt Jessica, absentmindedly. I knew her well enough to appreciate her mind was on other things. I'd have loved to have asked what she was thinking about, but Paula was still in full flow.

'I didn't have time to look at today's itinerary this morning. Do either of you know what's next on the agenda, a tour of the city? Looks a fascinating place. Very different from Tehran.'

There was no time to chat with Aunt Jessica once we'd eaten. After a brief trip to our rooms to unpack and sort ourselves out, we were back on the coach.

'Our first visit will be to the Friday Mosque, the most important monument in the city. This area didn't come under Muslim rule until the seventh century and Zoroastrianism continued to be the dominant religion here for the next hundred years. The original mosque was built in 1350 but it's been added to over the centuries.'

Despite Aahil's description, nothing had prepared us for the sheer size of the whole complex. We stood in the centre of an enclosed central square gazing up at the huge portico that dominated the entrance to the main mosque. Aunt Jessica told us that this particular architectural feature was to be found all Iranian mosques. Inside the place was a rabbit warren of passages and side rooms around the main prayer hall.

'The others have all moved on. You're going to get left behind if you don't hurry up and take that shot,' said Aunt Jessica.

'I know,' I wailed, 'But this is the perfect spot back here with the light coming through those pillars at just the right angle to cast interesting shadows on the courtyard beyond. Trouble is. every time I wait for people to move on, another group comes in before I can get a clear shot.'

Back in the main square, we were given a quarter of an hour to look round and take photos before meeting up again at the far corner. Inevitably the time disappeared, and when I looked at my watch, I realised I was already late. By now the courtyard was, if not exactly crowded, full of groups of tourists. It didn't help that they were aimlessly milling about staring up at the spectacular buildings and totally oblivious of my attempt to weave my way through.

'Sorry, sorry, sorry,' I panted. 'Lost track of time.'

'No problem,' said Aahil. 'You're not the last. We're still waiting for another couple of people.'

After a few more minutes, two or three of the others began to get restless. Sensing their mood, Aahil said, 'While we're waiting for the others, let me tell you a bit more about where we're going next. It's an Iranian tradition that the Friday Mosque is built next to the bazaar so that everyone can attend for noon prayers. Kerman's Grand Bazaar is one of the oldest trading centres in Iran, and it stretches for twelve hundred metres northeast to…'

'Here comes Caroline,' interrupted Irene.

She put an arm round the clearly distressed woman. 'What on earth's the matter?'

'I can't find Robert. He went off to find a toilet. I waited where he said, but he didn't come back.'

CHAPTER 12

'Not to worry,' I said. 'You go with Aahil and the others while I go back and find him.'

That was easier said than done. The public conveniences were in the far corner of the square but there was no sign of Robert inside. Nor was he at the spot where Caroline had said the two of them were supposed to meet. I wandered around in the general area and eventually spotted him half-hidden inside an arch in the colonnade. At least I assumed it was him. The man had his back to me, but he was wearing a similar navy fleece to the one I'd noticed Robert wearing earlier. I shouted his name and he turned, stuffing his mobile into his pocket. I waved an arm and once he'd spotted me, he hurried over.

'We were getting worried about you,' I said.

'Sorry,' he mumbled as we traversed the square. 'Lost track of time.'

Considering it was now twenty minutes later than the pre-arranged meeting time after what had been intended as a short comfort stop, it seemed a pretty poor excuse, but I didn't bother question it.

It had taken me so long to find Robert that I was concerned I'd have problems catching up with our main party. I needn't have worried. I'd seen them all heading down a street, and once we reached it, I was relieved to Aunt Jessica had held back to wait for us.

'Everyone else has gone into the tea house.'

I wondered where on earth she was taking us as we

descended into what appeared to be a basement, but it opened out into a magnificent large octagon-shaped vaulted chamber with what looked like a sunken ancient, blue-tiled bathing pool in the centre lit by a glass chandelier.

'Are you going to just stand there with your mouth open, or are you going to join us?'

'Sorry,' I muttered. 'Not quite what I expected.'

Aunt Jessica chuckled. 'It was one of the city's many bathhouses. The rest of us are over in the corner.'

I looked across to where she was pointing. Robert was already stepping onto the low raised platform that ran around the perimeter of the room. He clambered up onto a high deep divan and settled himself amongst the cushions next to his wife. The couch looked more like a giant bed on stilts than somewhere to sit to eat or drink. To judge from the expression on her face and the whispered exchange, it was going to take some time before marital harmony would be fully restored.

Unlike the rest of the Hamilton women, Aunt Jessica is tall, but even with her long legs, hoisting herself up onto the second high divan was still quite a challenge. I put out an arm to help. It might be the Iranian custom to eat their meals curled up in such a fashion, but none of our party looked particularly comfortable. Once the waiter had brought glasses of green tea in metal holders for us latecomers, I settled against the back of the divan and stretched out my legs in front of me.

'Here. Would you like one of these?'

Barbara handed me a small plate of what looked like small orange lollipops. 'They're sugar sticks. You're supposed to stir your tea with it.'

I swizzled one around in the steaming liquid. After a cautious sip, I decided it was sweet enough.

'What am I supposed to with this now?'

'We put ours back on the plate.'

Easier said than done. The plate had been returned to

the long trestle table. With my cup in one hand and the sugar stick in the other, I had to shuffle on my bottom to the front of the divan and lean across. Not exactly the most elegant of actions which Paula was quick to point out.

Suitably rested, we continued our tour wandering through the maze of small stalls lining the covered corridors of the Grand Bazaar. Though the decoration on the walls was hidden behind hanging goods, the ribbed arched ceiling was covered in a variety of intricate mosaic patterns. There was so much to take in.

'I love exploring bazaars,' I said sniffing the air. 'All the wonderful smells, exotic spices and the bright colours, the noise and all the bustle of crowds. The sheer exuberance of it all.'

'Did you know bazaar is originally a Persian word?' Aunt Jessica said.

'Really?' I put on my best interested voice though I was more concerned watching Caroline determinedly holding onto her husband's arm. Even when she had to let go for him to take a photo she stood resolutely by his side until he'd finished. Not that I blamed her. Despite everything there was that kept attracting my attention, I was careful to keep one eye on Aunt Jessica the whole time. The place was heaving and if I became separated, there was a good chance, I could be wandering around the maze of side passages for weeks before I was found again.

How Aahil managed to keep us all together is a mystery. He led us into yet another enclosed square, though this one had a garden area of sorts with a few small trees in the centre.

'We are going first into the ethnological museum built in what was an old bathhouse.'

To be honest, I'd had my fill of looking at old pots and bits of stone and sculpture, but after the first few rooms which were little more than alcoves along the route, the corridor opened up into a large octagonal bath chamber much like the one we'd been in earlier, but on a much grander scale. Around the central pool, were a series of deep alcoves like small open-sided rooms. Inside each one, were two or three life-sized manikins dressed as seventeenth century traders. The lower half of the walls were tiled but what caught my attention, were the ceilings with their elaborate exquisitely carved geometric plasterwork which Aahil referred to as squinches. A great word I remembered from my first trip with Aunt Jessica to Morocco. They had something to do with supporting the round base of a dome on the top of a square room.

The museum and baths were part of a preserved complex that also included a school, a caravanserai for the visiting traders, a mosque and a mint all arranged around the central square. The complex even had its own bazaar leading off one end.

It was a group of weary but very contented passengers who climbed down the coach steps when we returned to the hotel that evening. Even the suitably penitent Robert was back in favour with his wife.

Just inside the front entrance was a small coffee shop separated from the main lobby by tall plants on a low raised area.

'I'm dying for a drink. I'm going to have a coffee before I go up. Want to join me?' Aunt Jessica headed for the steps.

'I'll be there in a mo,' I called out after her. I turned to Aahil who was behind me.

'That was a great day.'

He smiled shyly. 'Good, I'm glad you enjoyed it.'

'Everyone did.'

He sighed. 'I hope so.'

'Is something wrong?'

He shook his head and began to follow the rest of the

group already making for the lifts. I put out a hand to stop him.

'Your boss isn't blaming you for what happened the other day, is he?'

I'd obviously hit a nerve because he turned his head and looked me in the eye.

'How's about you and I grab a coffee and you can tell me all about it?'

Before he could protest, I took him by the elbow and steered him to one side.

I pressed him again about his boss and he gradually opened up. 'He was furious with me for not letting him know about the accident immediately after it happened. It was Hassan who rang him at the end of the day to explain why the itinerary plans had been altered. He has to account for any changes.'

'But your boss didn't threaten you with the sack?'

'Nothing like that. Obviously, he was not very pleased and gave me a long lecture, but he calmed down eventually.'

'So, what's the problem?'

He gave a long sigh. 'I didn't actually see the accident. I heard the screech of brakes behind me. I turned and saw the body lying there in the road and suddenly all this screaming broke out. I just froze. When the police tried to move us on, it was one of the passengers who took charge. He gathered the party together and led us round the next corner.'

'It's no good blaming yourself. Lots of people freak out when something like that happens. I'm not that proud of the way I reacted either.'

'But several passengers have been passing comments. Even this morning I overheard a little group of them saying how useless I was.'

'Ignore them. They're not worth bothering about. You're a great guide. Just carry on, and in a day or two it will all be forgotten, you mark my words.'

He looked at me and smiled. 'Thanks.'

We continued talking for another few minutes. I thought a change of subject might take his mind off things and asked why he had decided to become a guide. He seemed a lot happier when I left him.

By the time I reached the coffee shop, I discovered Aunt Jessica wasn't alone. Barbara, and Mary and Gordon Hurley had joined her.

'What kept you? You've been gone ages.'

'Sorry about that. I was nattering with Aahil. You remember I told you about him studying in England?' She nodded. 'I was asking him all about it. Seems he did an engineering degree at Imperial College.'

'So why didn't he become an engineer when he came back to Iran?' asked Mary.

'Exactly. That's what I said. Apparently, all the available jobs were in the desert areas in the south a long way from Tehran. His father wasn't a well man, and his family needed him there. Eventually he did get a job, but it was way below the level of his qualifications, and he hated it. After eighteen months, he packed it in and decided to train as a guide. He said the pay is much better.'

'How interesting.'

'Then he asked me about my job. For some reason he thought I might be a hairdresser.'

Aunt Jessica spluttered as she drank her coffee then burst out laughing.

'What's so funny?'

She waved a hand and shook her head. 'I'll tell you later.'

It wasn't until we were back to her room that I brought up the subject again.

'What was so hilarious earlier about Aahil asking me if I was a hairdresser?'

She grinned. 'Let's put it like this, sweetie, he wasn't asking you what you did for a living.'

'I don't understand.'

'Obviously. He was asking you if you were gay.'

'What!'

'Hairdressers in Iran are the only gay members of the community that are tolerated in the country.'

'The way women can't be seen in public with their hair uncovered, I'm surprised they allow men to become hairdressers at all.'

'That's rather the point. Gay men are not considered real men.'

'That's appalling. Someone ought to do something about it.'

She gave a derisive snort. 'You can change the law, but laws won't stop people's attitudes. Anyway, you need to respect Iranian customs while you're here.'

'Aahil is an attractive guy. I don't deny it. I enjoy his company. But that is it. End of story. I'm not about to have a holiday fling!'

I stood up and strode to the door. I resisted the temptation to slam it as I left.

Aunt Jessica's attitude had taken me by surprise. She is no prude. In fact, she's the only one in the family who accepts me for who I am. Even my mother is convinced that one day I'll come to my senses and settle down "with a nice girl". True, I've never had a serious relationship. And, since I was summarily dismissed from the bank three years ago for conduct likely to bring the company into disrepute – on pretty dodgy evidence, I might add – I've not had a friendship of any kind. Things have been far too hectic for much of a social life since I moved to London.

CHAPTER 13

Our tour the next day promised to be different from anything we'd seen so far. We travelled out of the city into the desert to see an abandoned thousand-year-old citadel seemingly in the middle of nowhere.

Eventually we drove into a collection of unimpressive, low, one-storey, flat roofed buildings up on a slight rise where we could look down on the sand-coloured mudbrick fortress.

'With all those crenelated walls and round towers on the corners, it looks like a medieval castle from some blockbuster filmset rather than a real place,' I said. 'If you ignore the modern stuff dotted about, you can imagine that any minute now a band of armed knights will ride out from the gate and charge at us with lances at full tilt.'

Aunt Jessica chuckled. 'There speaks a true romantic.'

The coach drew up outside the main entrance gate and we all trooped off the coach and followed Aahil into the fortress. Close up, it was clear that although the front façade had been heavily restored, time and the weather had taken its toll on much of what remained. The place was not just a military bastion; within the high walls was an extensive settlement. More akin to Diocletian's Palace in Split than an English Norman castle.

'Until recently, it was the second largest mudbrick building in the world. The largest was its sister castle built not far away at Bam, but that was destroyed by an earthquake in 2003. We'll see the ruins in the distance on our way back,' explained Aahil.

Paula looked up from her notebook. She was the only one in the party who avidly took notes everywhere we went. 'Why build it out here in the middle of nowhere?'

'Both citadels were built on the Silk Road. The great wealth of the Sassanid empire that ruled Iran before the Arab conquest lay in trade. With that trade came new ideas and new skills so this citadel became a thriving city not only trading in valuable goods and quality textiles but developing its own craft industries. It even became a centre for sword and knife manufacture.'

In one or two places the original roof was intact, and we climbed up to take a closer look. Rather than the level surface I'd been expecting, it was covered in a regular pattern of low domes which made walking tricky, but the views stretching across the plain to the range of hills along the far horizon made it well worth the effort.

This was a good opportunity to take a photo looking down over the whole complex. I picked my way across to the edge and angled the camera to best capture the regular chequerboard of narrow passageways shaded by tall walls. I sensed rather than heard someone coming up behind me, but it wasn't until they spoke that I realised who it was.

'You and Aahil seem to be getting along. It's good to see he's beginning to pull himself together at long last, don't you think?'

I glared at Paula. 'Not everyone is quite as insensitive as you at seeing a mangled body lying in the street, especially when it was someone they knew, however briefly.'

'Ouch!'

It may have come out with more venom than I'd intended but I was not prepared to back down. 'As I recall, from all the screaming and pandemonium, Aahil was not the only one to be affected. Poor Mary was so traumatised it gave her a bad asthma attack. We were on the point of having to call an ambulance for her.'

Paula had the grace to look suitably contrite, but I didn't

stop to hear her excuses and turned to follow the others already making their way back to ground level.

When I eventually made it into the street, for a brief moment, I wasn't sure which way to turn. From the back, with their heads and shoulders draped in flowing scarves, it was virtually impossible to recognise any of the women in our party, but I spotted Gordon's Tilley sun hat off to the left.

When I eventually caught up with Aunt Jessica, she asked, 'Get any good photos up there? You were gone long enough.'

'Not as many as I'd have liked,' I muttered.

'Oh. What happened?'

'Tell you later.'

Rayan Citadel was a major tourist attraction not only for foreign visitors but also for locals and coming towards us was a party of ten or so young Iranian women. As they approached, their guide, who looked not much older than the others, stopped us.

'You speak English?'

When we all nodded, she told us she was an English teacher, and that the girls were her students. She explained they would love the chance to practice their English if we wouldn't mind talking to them. They were all so eager that we were all only too happy to spend a few minutes with them. I ended up taking lots of group shots.

Our next stop was to some gardens which lay – surprise, surprise – behind yet another set of high brick walls.

I was getting peckish and as the coach drove past the entrance, I noticed a couple of stalls by the side of the gate. As the last of the group were getting off, I hurried over to see if there were any snacks I could buy. They both turned out to be book stalls selling glossy guides of the major tourist cities, Persian art and architecture as well as of the gardens we were about to see.

'I don't suppose there's any chance of getting something

to eat inside is there? I'm starving,' I asked Aunt Jessica when I caught up with her again.

I'm not sure if it was because he'd overheard my question but, before she could answer, Aahil announced to everyone that lunch had been booked for us in the restaurant at the top of the gardens.

'Shahzadeh Garden means the Prince's Garden and it's been remodelled by successive rulers over the years.'

We all followed him at a slow but steady pace up the long gently rising path alongside the series of stepped lakes that formed the spine of the long narrow historic Persian garden. Above us, I could just make out an ornate arched building in the distance which I assumed was where we would eat.

'We'll have worked up quite an appetite by the time we get there,' joked Mary.

Everyone took their time admiring the line of fountains that ran down the centre and the narrow flanking flower beds, but Aahil urged us not to stop for photos as there would be plenty of time on our way back down.

Lunch was served outside on the wide terrace at the back of the building. The restaurant was obviously popular because all the tables appeared to be taken, not just by coach parties of tourists like us, but also by what appeared to be extended family groups of the locals complete with plenty of young children happily running around.

A long table, mercifully at the edge, had been reserved for us and before long, bowls of steaming soup were placed in front of us. Before we'd even had a chance to drink it, a range of dishes were laid out down the centre for us to serve ourselves. Though most people were happy to take a portion of everything, I was more wary. I do like to know what I'm eating.

'This is minced beef topped with yogurt.' Aunt Jessica handed me a plate.

The sliced tomato was easy to recognise though the herbs sprinkled on top were harder to identify. I wasn't too sure about another dish of what I was told was a chickpea concoction though I'll admit it turned out to be very tasty.

As I helped myself to another portion, Helen, the retired teacher from Gravesend, asked, 'Have you tried the aubergine? It's delicious. You need to get some before it all goes.'

'To be honest, it's not my favourite vegetable.'

'Then you don't like moussaka, I take it?'

'Actually, I make a pretty mean moussaka, though I say it myself.'

'A man who cooks!'

'I'll have you know I'm a professional sous chef!'

We discovered we both loved working in the kitchen. I told her about my time in Mario's Trattoria and it turned out since her retirement Helen had signed on for a "More Adventurous Cooking" evening course at her local college. Before long we were swapping recipes.

At the end of the meal, everyone started to drift off. We were free to wander back down to the entrance gate at the bottom in our own time.

'I'm just off to join the inevitable long queue outside the ladies,' Aunt Jessica informed me. 'It could take ages so don't bother to wait for me. You go down when you're ready and we'll meet up at the gate.'

'Okey-dokey. I was planning on taking lots of photos, so you'll probably beat me to it anyway.'

I took my time finishing my coffee chatting with Helen and Phil. I confess I had an ulterior motive. I wanted to see if I could catch Aahil by himself. I was still worried about him after our last chat and wanted to give him a bit of moral support, but after Aunt Jessica's warning, decided it probably wasn't a good idea anyway.

CHAPTER 14

In any case, Aahil was nowhere to be seen in the restaurant area or in the men's toilets. I spent several minutes in front of the summerhouse taking pictures down the flight of long rectangular lakes trying to catch the rainbow effect of the sun shining through the falling water from the line of fountains.

Eventually, I realised it was time to start making tracks. I decided to take the path on the other side from the one we came up. I hadn't gone too far when I heard rapid footsteps coming down behind me. I was half turned, taking a photo at the time, but I saw Paula out of the corner of my eye. She'd already tried to catch me a couple of times since our spat at Rayen Castle, but I wasn't ready to hear her apology just yet. Let her feel guilty for a bit longer.

A few feet away, Irene was sitting on a stone bench admiring the view and I hurried to join her.

'Spectacular, isn't it?'

She smiled. 'And even with all the people, it's so peaceful.'

We talked about inconsequential things, the nice lunch, the pretty flower borders and the dense tall trees that bounded the garden, but she was still looking very pale and far from her normal bubbly state.

'I still can't stop thinking about the accident,' she said out of the blue.

'It affected us all.'

'Yes but…'

I waited, but whatever she was about to say, she thought better of it.

'We certainly fit a lot into each day,' said Barbara when we walked into the hotel at the end of our day's outing. 'It seems like days ago when we were chatting with all those lovely girls at the fortress, but it was only this morning! It's been so full on all afternoon.'

'I know what you mean,' I agreed.

'But I wouldn't have wanted to miss out on that beautiful shrine to that Sufi saint. I'll never remember his name, but it was fascinating about him being the founder of the Dervishes. Wasn't that mosque beautiful?'

'There goes one happy customer,' I said to Aunt Jessica as we watched Barbara bustle away towards the lifts.

'Did you enjoy the day?'

'Very much. Though I agree with Barbara. I can't believe just how much we've seen in so short a time. I've taken hundreds of photos. I tried to get some shots through the coach window of the two minarets sticking up like turquoise pencils in the distance as we approached that shrine Barbara was just talking about. I'm dying to transfer them to my laptop. With a bit of luck, when we get home, I'll be able to get rid of the window reflection with a bit of photoshopping.'

The doors on one lift were just closing as we arrived but we pressed the call button, and another arrived almost straightaway. We had it to ourselves as we travelled up to our floor.

'So are you going to tell me what made you so annoyed earlier when we were at the citadel?'

'Oh that,' I shrugged. 'It was nothing really.'

'Bad enough for you to glower at everyone else for the next ten minutes including those delightful young students. What did Paula say that fired you up so much? I noticed the two of you deep in conversation just before I came down from the roof.'

Aunt Jessica wasn't happy at me spending so much time with Aahil, so I thought it best not to mention Paula's snide remarks about my attraction to our good-looking young guide.

'She was talking about the accident again. I've never met anyone quite so cold-hearted. She doesn't seem to understand how many of us were quite traumatised witnessing the death of someone we knew.'

'I suppose it's because her journalist instincts took over, looking for a story.'

'A man died in a hit and run. End of story,' I snapped.

The lift doors slid open with a faint hiss, and I stepped out and headed down the corridor, but Aunt Jessica matched my stride and kept pace by my side.

'Why didn't the car stop?' I muttered.

'I have no idea. There could be any number of reasons.'

We'd reached my room and I went in, but she followed me inside.

'Or, as I believe you said earlier, it was no accident and that someone deliberately intended to kill Yusef Kaya.'

'But you didn't agree,' I protested.

'As I recall, my exact words were, "we shall have to find out more about our mysterious fellow passenger". I'm still not convinced it was a deliberate attempt to kill him, but I'm prepared to admit I think there's a whole lot more to his death than a simple accident. Something is definitely going on and I'm as keen as you to get to the heart of it.'

She sat down on my bed.

'You're right,' I said. 'I'm sorry. That woman made me so worked up, but that's no excuse for taking it out on you.'

I sank down next to her and sighed.

'I don't suppose you've learnt any more from those scribbled notes at the back of the itinerary booklet?'

She tapped the side of her nose. 'That's what I've been trying to tell you. Because they were in pencil, they weren't very clear in the first place and I had to try several times, I managed to get a couple of photos last night and emailed them to a Turkish colleague of mine at the British Museum. He sent me a text message late this afternoon. According to him, they're not Turkish. He thinks they're probably Farsi. He wanted to know if I'm happy for him to show them to an Iranian friend.'

'I trust you said yes?'

She laughed. 'What do you think?'

CHAPTER 15

Irene was sitting at a table by herself when we came down to breakfast and, although I'd been hoping to have a private chat with Aunt Jessica, it would have been rude not to join her. It wasn't long before Mary and Gordon came to join us.

'You look a little heavy-eyed this morning, Mary,' said Aunt Jessica. 'Did you have a bad night?'

'I'm not sleeping that well I have to admit. Every time I close my eyes, I see this picture of Yusef flying through the air.' She gave an involuntary shudder.

Irene shook her head. 'I didn't actually see what happened. I was looking over my shoulder when he stepped into the road. Yusef was just in front of me as we were walking down the road and suddenly, he just stopped. I'd have bumped straight into him if I hadn't stepped to the side. But I can sympathise, Mary. I can still hear that dreadful crunch as the car hit him and the screech of brakes of the oncoming vehicle.'

I felt Aunt Jessica's knee nudge mine beneath the table as if to say, 'Told you there'd be an innocent explanation.'

Out loud, she said, 'Shall we talk about something a little less stressful? Off to Shiraz today. At least you'll be able to catch up on your sleep on the journey, Mary.'

'Those seats are very comfortable aren't they,' I agreed.

Irene nodded. 'It will be quite nice to have a bit of a rest today. Everything has been a little full-on so far.'

The other three left before us giving Aunt Jessica and me

a chance to talk over how we could solve the riddle of the mysterious Yusef and what he was up to.

'What's the next step? Do we have to wait until your Turkish friend gets back to you about the writing in Yusef's booklet?'

Aunt Jessica stirred her tea, deep in thought. 'It would help if we knew if there has been any developments in finding the car that ran Yusef down.'

'That's a pretty tall order, especially now we've left Tehran.'

She nodded. 'Even if the police have found it, they're hardly likely to report the details in the local papers. In any case, even if we could find copies online, they'd all be in Farsi. The only thing I can think of is to ask Aahil if he's heard anything. What's that frown for?'

'I'd be a bit apprehensive about bringing up anything to do with the accident with him. According to Miss Know-all Paula, he was pretty shaken up at the time.'

'Wasn't everyone?'

'Yes,' I said tentatively. 'But according to Paula, he was still in such a bad way that even after the police said they were free to leave, someone else had to phone for the coach to take them back to the hotel. I'm not so sure it would be a good idea to remind Aahil about it.'

'He did sound a bit fraught when I called him from the shop,' she conceded.

I shrugged. 'He may not know in any case?'

'But Hassan or Ali might. They must be in touch with their families and must be just as curious as we are.'

'But are you sure they understand enough English for us to ask?'

'I doubt it. Which is why we need Aahil's help.'

Friday was essentially a travel day. The distance between Kerman and Yazd was almost two hundred miles, but the good news was that we would stop at Saryazd Castle on the way.

Aunt Jessica had warned me when she'd first invited me on the trip that Iran was a huge country and moving between the major archaeological and ancient cultural centres would involve some long journeys. At the time, I was so excited at the thought of visiting some of the fabulous cities I'd seen on a recent television series about Persia that it hadn't bothered me.

As I followed her out of the breakfast room back up to our rooms, my spirits began to sag. Not only was I worried about Aahil's reaction – what Aunt Jessica didn't seem to understand was that he was a sensitive soul – the prospect of having to spend so much time trapped in the coach did nothing to lighten my mood. The only bright spot was the comfortable seats and extra space between each row.

It didn't take long to pack my stuff. Apart from an extra sweater, the only thing I needed to take inside the coach was my camera. Everything else could go in my grip in the luggage compartment.

When I went next door, though Aunt Jessica's case was packed, her bed was covered with piles of cardboard folders as well as all the projection equipment.

'Do you really need all this stuff on the journey?'

'There's no reason why we can't put the equipment in the boot. The laptop and projector are in their cases, so they won't come to any harm. There's a cloth shopping bag around somewhere. Can you shove all the handouts in it while I get my coat and arrange my scarf? Then we can take the cases down.'

I knew Aunt Jessica was planning to give one of her talks on the coach on each of the three long travel days – it had meant I only had three presentations to prepare for the whole trip which, given how busy I was with my own business right now, was great – but I was curious why one lecture should involve such a wodge of stuff. I picked up the first folder and looked inside.

'That one's just a collection of interesting articles that people might like to read on the journey,' she explained.

As always, Aunt Jessica and I were last onto the coach. As there were so many spare seats available, Robert and Caroline had already decided to sit separately so they could each have a seat by a window. As this was my first visit to Iran, Aunt Jessica was always happy to let me take the window seat in any case.

Before long everyone had settled themselves and we were off. Once we'd left the built-up area, Aahil announced that the women could remove their scarfs but whenever we approached any of the frequent police checks, they would have to cover their heads again.

The major roads were metalled but few stretches were more than a single carriageway and I don't remember seeing anything that approached a Western-style service station. When it came time for a coffee stop, the coach pulled off the main road and drew up alongside a four-foot-high wall on the edge of a small village. Ali laid out a line of cups along the top which Hassan filled from a large vacuum flask. We helped ourselves to coffee and fig biscuits.

Paula made a beeline to speak to me and this time, there was no way I could avoid her.

'I'm sorry I upset you yesterday. I was only trying to make conversation and I'm not sure quite what I said to cause such a reaction.'

'Forget it,' I muttered. I knew I was behaving like an adolescent harbouring my grudge because of her comments about Aahil. Especially when they'd been justified, and I couldn't deny his reaction to the accident had been unprofessional. Nonetheless, I turned back to the packet of biscuits and took another, hoping she would take the hint.

'What I wanted to ask you was what you thought about Yusef. There was something about him that struck me as odd.'

'Oh?' Against my better judgement I was intrigued.

'As I understand it, the accident happened because Yusef stepped off the path when he was answering his phone and not paying attention to the traffic.'

'So?'

'Tourists don't usually receive phone calls in the middle of the day. Even businessmen who like to keep in touch, tend to arrange calls for later in the evening. I know it was only the start of the holiday, but he didn't even pretend to show any interest in what we were there to see and, as far as I could tell, he made little effort to speak to any of the rest of us. Kept himself to himself.'

'Perhaps he was shy.'

The scathing look she gave me would have soured honey.

There was no time to talk further with Paula as Hassan and Ali had cleared away the coffee cups and everyone was getting back on the coach.

'Saryazd castle dates to the Sassanid dynasty between the third to seventh century AD. Like Rayen citadel we saw yesterday, it was built using mud bricks. Once you get off the coach, you might like to have your cameras ready. Once we get nearer, you might see something interesting in the deep moat which surrounds the concentric wall.'

Intrigued by Aahil's suggestion, everyone hurried off the coach and started walking the short distance from the carpark to the entrance. The moat was dry, but it was deep, and it wasn't until we reached the edge and look down that we could see the camels. I could see three on this side of the drawbridge and there were possibly more on the other. Aahil was right in that they, or at least their decorative trappings, were well worth a photo or two. I was particularly pleased with a closeup of a headshot. Not only had I captured the headdress covered in brightly-coloured, woollen tassels threaded with blue beads to ward off the evil eye, and the cowbells, but best of all, the lofty, disdained expression on the animal's face and the way it held its neck was exactly what you'd expect on a fashion model in some glossy magazine.

Inside the first narrow chamber, the wall was covered with notice boards in English and what I presumed was Farsi and Arabic. Once Aahil had given us a little more information about the place, we were free to explore on our own. The whole place was far more degraded than the earlier adobe citadel and though we passed several sets of steps up to the second floor, I was wary of trying any of them. Eventually, several of the more adventurous members of the party found a route up. Some steps had disappeared, and it was only those with long enough legs that managed to make it to the top. I wandered around for a bit then tackled the tricky climb up the badly eroded steps to the third storey. I managed to get some good shots over the complex and a couple looking down on Barbara and Mary who had decided to stay below.

Just as I was contemplating going back down, I spotted Paula on a narrow ledge leaning back against a wall to steady herself as she snapped away with her camera. I felt a bit guilty at the way I'd shunned her earlier. Possibly, I'd jumped to the wrong conclusion when she'd talked about Aahil. On reflection, perhaps it really had only been a throwaway comment as a prelude to talking about Yusef. It wouldn't do any harm to get her take on our mysterious Turk either.

'Hi,' I said when she put her camera down.

She looked a little surprised as she obviously hadn't heard my approach.

'I was thinking about what you said about Yusef,' I went on. 'If he wasn't here for a holiday, what do you think he was up to?'

'Well, just between you and me, don't spread it around, I wondered if it might be something to do with drugs.'

'Drugs!'

She nodded. 'I was genning up on stuff about Persia on the internet just before we came away and quite by chance,

I came upon this article about the last Shah's twin sister. Seems she was arrested at Geneva airport in 1960 with a suitcase containing several kilos of heroin and then there was a big furore when several leading French newspapers published the story some ten years later. She tried to bring an injunction against them and even the American government became involved. Anyway, that had me digging a bit more and I discovered Iran has one of the highest rates of drug addiction in the world and that trafficking is a major issue in the country even today.'

'If you say so, but isn't it a bit of a leap to think Yusef was over here to buy drugs?'

'I was thinking more along the lines of him setting up some kind of supply network back to the UK. It might explain all those phone calls. Perhaps it was his contact.'

CHAPTER 16

We arrived in Yazd around four o'clock. Our hotel was what I assumed was a converted farm. It was a small family-run business and I doubt the place had more than a dozen rooms at best, so with Aahil and the two drivers, we probably filled the place. We were shown into a sitting-room and served with tea while our cases were unloaded and put outside our doors.

Our two rooms were in what was probably an old barn, or some sort of storehouse attached to the main building. Mine was very different in shape to Aunt Jessica's, but both were comfortably converted. The smaller one, which I took, was an ensuite twin with room for two single beds and the minimum of furniture. Aunt Jessica's was a large family room that extended back twice as far as mine. It had a double bed at either end of a central sitting area plus a single along the side wall tucked under the wide set of steps which led to a sizeable mezzanine area with another double bed.

'We could hold a party for everyone in here,' I said.

By the time we'd taken in the cases and freshened up, there was no chance to even unpack. We'd been told to be back in twenty minutes ready for a drive into the centre to see the main square and the mosque lit up before dinner.'

Lit up against the midnight blue of the sky behind, the main façade of the mosque stretched across the whole width of one end of the square. It was perfectly symmetrical with two tall minarets rising either side of the large vaulted central entrance flanked by two storeys of smaller units. It would have been a perfect picture with the subtle pale blue-grey lighting in the centre and soft orange in the side arches were it not for all the metal barrier rails stacked right across the top of the square.

'What are they for?' Barbara was the first to ask.

'They are obviously getting ready for a big event here in the near future. A rally of some kind, I expect.'

'Is it anything to do with the banners?'

On one side of the square, half a dozen huge portraits of important-looking men – mostly clerics – printed on fabric hung over the buildings.

'I recognise the faces of those two, but I couldn't tell you who they are,' said Phil.

'The one in the black turban is Ayatollah Ali Khamenei the Supreme Leader, and the one to the right is President Hassan Rouhani,' Aahil explained. 'The others are members of parliament or on the Guardian Council.'

'Ali and Hassan! Same as our drivers.' Mary clapped her hands. 'We're being driven by the great and the good!'

Phil had more serious matters on his mind. 'I thought Iran was a theocracy, but I was reading an article in the flight magazine coming over that the President is a democratically elected office.'

'That's true. The President is elected every four years. He can serve a further four if elected, but Rouhani will retire next year, and we will vote for a new president.'

'Is it only the Supreme Leader allowed to wear a black turban? The others all seem to be wearing white ones.'

Ali shook his head. 'The black turban is only worn by clerics who are the direct descendants of the Prophet Muhammad.'

Ever since lunch time, I'd been itching to tell Aunt Jessica about my conversation with Paula and once we were back at the hotel and we could talk in private, I wasted no time.

'So, what do you think of Paula's suggestion?'

'That Yusef was involved in some sort of heroin trafficking? I confess it wasn't an idea that had occurred to me. I knew about the drug smuggling, of course.'

'Paula thinks that's why Yusef was making all these phone calls.'

She looked thoughtful. 'It's possible I suppose, but I don't think we should jump to any conclusions just yet. Right now, I think it's time we joined the others, or we'll be late for dinner.

Not surprisingly for such a small establishment, dinner was a set meal. When I asked what was in the stew being ladled into my plate the only answer the young man gave me was a smile.

I pointed to the contents of my plate and said again, 'What is this?'

He may not have understood English, but he sussed my meaning and said, 'Ghormeh sabzi.'

I wasn't any wiser, but Aahil came to my rescue. 'You could say it's our national dish. The traditional Persian recipe is kidney beans and a mixture of herbs and dark bitter greens such as spinach and leeks and spring onions, but this one also has beef.'

Steaming bowls of rice were laid down the centre of the long table for us to help ourselves. The greenish tinge to the dark brown concoction in my plate looked none too appetising as far as I was concerned, but those around me made appreciative noises, so I heaped some rice on top and took a mouthful. I can't say it was by any means my favourite dish I'd had so far but neither was it the worst.

Over dinner, Helen asked Aahil about his family.

'I have two older brothers and a sister.'

'Does that mean you're the baby in the family?'

Aahil laughed. 'Not quite. My brother Naasah has a three-year-old daughter. She is spoilt by everyone in the house. But she will soon have her nose pushed out of joint, as you English say, because Tahib's wife is expecting a baby in January.'

'You all live together?'

'It is customary in Iran. When a son gets married, he brings his new wife to join the family.'

'Doesn't the house get a bit crowded?'

Attractive dimples appeared in his cheeks as he smiled. 'No. The house gets bigger. We build more rooms. But when my sister gets married, she will move to live with her husband's family.'

I was dying to ask if he was married, but I knew it was best to stay silent.

We started talking amongst ourselves and it was only when I heard the word Yusef above the general murmur of conversation that my ears pricked up again. From the snatches I managed to catch I had the impression Paula was asking Aahil if he'd heard any more about the police investigation into the accident. They were both sitting at the far end of the table, and I couldn't hear much of his answer over the general chatter. Something about not finding the car.

I glanced across at Aunt Jessica sitting opposite who appeared to be listening to Barbara's lengthy tale of an incident on one of her previous holidays, but something in her expression told me Aahil's update on what had been happening in Tehran had not gone unnoticed.

At the end of the meal our plates were cleared away and although nothing was said, the waiter, who I took to be the son of the family, and his mother waited just inside the door.

'I think they are waiting to lay up for breakfast,' said Aunt Jessica.

Deprived of the chance to chat with fellow guests, everyone began to drift back to their respective rooms but my suspicions about Aunt Jessica earwigging the conversation at the far end of the table were confirmed when she waited until Paula passed her chair then slipped in behind her.

By the time I arrived outside, the two were chatting away. I decided to hang back. They stopped when they reached Paula's door, so I had no choice but to continue on.

I didn't have to wait long. I'd only just made it to my room and switched on the light when I heard Aunt Jessica's footsteps outside.

I raised an eyebrow as she stepped inside pulling the door closed behind her. 'Have the police caught anyone yet?'

'If they are questioning anyone, they're not making it public.'

I gave a shrug. 'On the plus side, it saves us asking, I suppose.'

'True. Best not to indicate what we're up to more than we have already.'

'It's not even nine o'clock,' I said, glancing at my watch. 'What do you want to do?'

'It'll give us the chance to do a bit of investigation. Do you have the hotel log-in for the internet?'

'I wrote it down when we first arrived but I'm not sure where I put it.'

'When you find it, come and join me next door.'

It took longer to find than I'd anticipated. My room was a bit of a mess. I'd dumped all my hand luggage on the spare bed. I eventually found the scrap of paper in the side pocket of my camera case where I'd put it for safe keeping.

I knocked and went straight in. She was sitting on her bed at the far end of the room with her mobile held to her ear. I went over to the sitting area and made myself comfy in one of the easy chairs.

'Take care. Speak to you soon.' She ended the call and came to join me.

'That was quick. Was that your Iranian friend from the British Museum?'

She shook her head. 'I rang to see how Maud was doing now she's home.'

'Was she still up? Did you manage to speak to her?'

'There's a three-and-a-half-hour time difference! Anyway, she's fine. Told me in no uncertain terms not to bother to check up on her every day. She doesn't want to hear from us for at least a week.'

'Sounds like she's back to her old self.'

'I also spoke to your mother. The nurse went in to see Maud this morning and was pleased with her progress and she assured me that between her, Edwina and the carer they are coping very well so we're not to worry.'

'That's good news. I hope you sent them all my love.'

'Of course. Now let's get on. Have you found that log-in?'

Her laptop was already open and waiting on a small table.

We began by looking up sites related to drugs in Iran. There was far more than I thought possible. When Paula had talked about the problem, I'd assumed that she'd exaggerated the situation to catch my attention but apparently not. If anything, several of the articles painted an even bigger problem. Though it seems that drugs were not the only thing traffickers were interested in.

'I know you can't take anything you read on Wikipedia as gospel, but it says here that "Iranian women are trafficked internally for the purpose of forced prostitution and for forced marriages to settle debts" and it talks about alcohol smuggling. It's a good job Mum and the aunts don't surf the net. They'd have fifty fits if they saw this.'

We looked at several more articles.

'What about this story Paula mentioned about the arrest of the Shah's sister?'

There was plenty to read through including a copy from a declassified telegram from the US State Department.

'This one's fascinating,' she said. 'Claims Ashraf Pahlavi was the real power behind the throne. She, rather than her brother, was the prime mover in involving the CIA in the 1953 coup which led to her brother taking the throne.'

'It says she persuaded her brother to set up SAVAK. What's that?'

'With the help of the CIA, the Shah set up his own secret police. It was brutal and had unlimited powers. The slightest criticism of the Shah's regime led to arrest and vicious torture. Dissidents were executed without trial. They even sent investigators to keep surveillance on Iranians abroad especially in Britain, the US, and France, where there were large numbers of students on government scholarships.'

'Good lord. No wonder so many fled the country.'

CHAPTER 17

On the coach the previous day on our journey to Yazd, Aahil had spoken a little about the major differences between Sunni Islam and the Shia Islam practiced in Iran and neighbouring Iraq and Azerbaijan. His explanation complemented Aunt Jessica's talk which covered the main religions practised historically during the different dynasties in the country. It was an excellent preparation for our first visit of the day to the abandoned Towers of Silence just outside the city where the people were laid to rest.

'According to Zoroastrian belief, dead bodies were considered unclean and were not allowed to pollute the sacred elements of water, earth, or fire and consequently could not be buried or cremated. Originally, the dead were placed at the top of hills in desert areas far from the villages to be scavenged by vultures. Later, as the population increased, they built tall towers just outside the villages where the bodies could be laid out on top, open to the skies but out of sight of the people.'

'Nice!' Helen drew out the word into two long syllables, her tone matching the distaste evident on her face. It produced titters of laughter from those around her.

'As you can see in the distance,' Aahil continued once everyone was quiet again, 'There are two towers. They served several villages in the area and as we make our way over, you'll see the small buildings where the families stayed for the ceremonies. Fifty years ago, they were both closed so today Zoroastrians are buried in a graveyard over in that direction. I'll point them out to you when we get to the top of the tower. The graves are lined with cement to prevent the bodies coming in contact with the earth.'

'That funny domed-shaped one has a couple of wind catcher towers,' said Phil.

Aahil smiled. 'Any guesses as to what it might be?'

'A water cistern.' Trust Paula to know the answer.

'Exactly. Yazd is in the middle of the desert. The wind catchers are vital to keep the water below cool.'

We slowly ambled across the site towards the towers. The closer we went, the higher the hills appeared to be. Climbing up was going to be a challenge.

'We are lucky that a set of steps were built five years ago so we no longer have to clamber up the hillside.'

The broad steps wound round the hillside, but they were still steep.

'How on earth did the older family members manage to get up to the top? They must have been fit,' said Mary as we waited for the late comers to catch up.

Aahil shook his head. 'The families remained here at the bottom. Once the body was washed and wrapped it was carried up by the priests. Only they entered the tower. I'll explain what happened inside when we get there. Take your time coming up. I'll wait for you.'

Inevitably the group became spread out. I took a couple of stops, resting against the waist- high side wall to admire the view. Being the youngest and relatively fit, I was one of the first to reach the semi-circular terrace at the base of the tower itself. Predictably, so was Paula.

She brushed back the hair whipping around her face, tucking it under her scarf that had come off on the way up. 'Do you think that they are the graves Aahil was talking about?'

I turned to look where she was pointing. 'That row of white lines beyond the wall over to the left?' I zoomed in with the camera. 'I think you're right.'

'Mary looks as though she's struggling. All those steps must be a challenge if you're an asthmatic.' For once, she seemed quite sympathetic to someone else's problems.

'She's not giving up though.'

I wondered if Paula would bring up the subject of Yusef being over here to buy drugs again, but she seemed more interested in taking photos of the distant outskirts of the city and the abandoned buildings below. Before long, she decided to go up the final set of steps up to the wooden door into the tower itself.

'You coming?'

'You go on up. I'll wait for my aunt.'

The next person to arrive was Robert. He gave me a quick nod and headed straight up. Caroline appeared a short time later. She stood huffing and puffing, leaning over the wall to get her breath back.

'You okay?' I asked.

She nodded. 'I hurried up that last bit to catch up with Robert.'

'He's already gone up to the top.'

She didn't say it, but I had the impression from her frown that she was not best pleased with the way her husband was treating her on this holiday. 'It's alright for him with those long legs of his, but when you're a shortie like me and you have to lift your knees to ninety degrees each time, those steps are a real killer.'

The first thing that struck me when I eventually went inside the tower was how quiet it was. The high walls provided shelter from the strong winds that had been roaring in my ears for the last half-hour. I said as much to Aunt Jessica.

'Why do you think they're called Towers of Silence?'

There wasn't a lot to see inside. In the centre of the stone paved floor was a large circular hole.

'When the bodies were brought in, they were unwrapped and laid out in concentric rings. Men in the outer ring, then women and finally the children in the centre. The priests would return after the bones had been picked clean by vultures. The bones were washed then dropped into the well.'

'What was to stop the bodies being scavenged by wild animals?' Trust Robert to come up with that one. The man appeared to be devoid of any sensitivity.

'The door was always kept firmly closed and the walls are too high to be scaled.'

It was another hectic day. Once we were back in Yazd, there were visits to the Friday Mosque, the water museum and a traditional henna mill – a tiny, incredibly dusty place where the leaves were ground by a large mill wheel driven originally by a donkey. It wasn't until we arrived at the Persian Gardens on our next stop that I had an opportunity to speak privately to Aunt Jessica. Even then I had to curb my impatience because before we were given free time to explore the gardens by ourselves, Aahil led us towards the squat octagonal pavilion in the centre. It was not a particularly large building though the same could not be said of the tall tower that rose from its centre which was twice as high as the building itself. The top half consisted of a series of long narrow openings.

'Any idea what all those sticks are for?' said a voice next to me.

I looked up at the thin, twig-like rods that stuck out from each of the tower's eight faces before turning to Gordon.

'Not a clue. They don't exactly look like part of the decoration, do they? Let's ask Aahil.'

Before we could reach him, Aahil had disappeared into the building.

'Dowlat-Abad Garden is a UNESCO World Heritage site and known as the Jewel of Yazd. It was laid out two hundred years ago.'

As Aahil continued, it wasn't just my eagerness to talk to

Aunt Jessica that made me wish he'd hurry up. I was rapidly beginning to get cold. No one else seemed bothered so I decided not to complain.

'You remember before we came in, I pointed out the wind catcher. The tower is thirty-three metres tall and it's the tallest wind catcher in the world. Follow me over here and I'll show you how it works.'

He led the way to the side of the room just behind me and stepped through the open doorway into a small room with what I took to be an empty pool. He took out a tissue and held it up to the ceiling. The moment he released it, it was whisked up into one of the vents and out of sight only to float back down again several feet away a few seconds later.

'The open vents at the top of the tower catch the wind which is drawn down into the building to refresh the air inside the house forcing the stale warm air in the room below to be sucked up the adjacent chimney.'

'No wonder I was getting so cold,' I muttered when I realised I'd been standing in the doorway catching the full effect of the downdraught on the back of my neck.

'It's so peaceful here, don't you think?' asked Aunt Jessica as we strolled by the side of the long pool that ran down to the centre the gardens outside.

At the far end, I took my time setting up the camera to take the perfect shot of the whole length of the pond flanked by lines of tall pine trees leading up to the distant building with its high wind tower rising in the centre of the picture.

By the time I'd finished the others had all moved on.

'You know we were looking at all those articles on the Shah's secret police force last night and the CIA involvement,' I said tentatively. 'It had me thinking earlier. Could it be that...?'

'Go on.'

'I was wondering about Robert.'

She could barely hide her smile. 'You can't imagine he's CIA?'

The whole idea sounded ridiculous now it was said out loud.

'Not exactly,' I said, thinking fast. 'But I did wonder if he'd been here before. He does seem to know a lot about Iran.'

'Oh?'

'Take the buffet meal the other day. When I asked him what was in the hot dish he'd just looked in, he said it was chelo kebab. Anyone else would have just said kebab. And he hadn't read the label.'

'Perhaps he has been before. Caroline did say he used to visit this part of the world on business before he retired.'

'Yes. But isn't it odd that he's never mentioned it?'

Our final visit was to the Fire Temple in the oldest part of the city.

'Zoroastrians have been worshipping at this spot for over seven hundred years.'

'But not in that building, presumably.' Gordon said what we were probably all thinking. There was nothing ancient-looking about the low clean modern lines of the temple in front of us.

Aahil smiled. 'True. The structure around the fire has had to be renovated many times over the years but I can assure you the temple you see now holding the holy fire resembles traditional Achaemenid architecture.'

I was listening with only half an ear as I tried to work out where best to stand to get a decent picture of the large circular pool surrounded by the picturesque apricot and almond trees without the rest of the group in the background.

'...Zoroastrianism is the oldest known monotheist religion. For a thousand years it was one of the most important religions in the world though today it has less than a hundred and nine thousand followers. Most live in

Iran though when the Arabs arrived bringing Islam, many fled to India and formed the Parsee community...'

Trying not to make it too obvious, I inched away from the group.

'...This is their main temple and followers come from all over the country to worship. It's one of the most holy places in the world for Zoroastrians. The equivalent of Mecca for Muslims or the Vatican for Roman Catholics...' Aahil was in full flow.

If I hadn't been so intent on sneaking away, I probably wouldn't have noticed them, but I wasn't the only one not paying attention. Robert and Caroline had distanced themselves behind the rest of the group. He was clutching his mobile and the tight-lipped expression on his wife's face left little doubt that she was far from happy with her husband. There was no noisy argument, but I had the distinct feeling she was giving him a good earbashing which was probably all the more effective for being delivered so coldly and quietly.

A few minutes later, the group began to move to the doors.

'As you go in,' said Aunt Jessica, 'I want you all to look up. At the very top of the building, you can see a beautiful Farvahar plaque picked out in blue showing the winged god, Ahura Mazda. You remember I talked about it on the coach yesterday.'

My attempts at a decent photo had not been that successful so I lingered until the last person disappeared through the doorway and took a couple more including the front of the building.

Inside, the corridor had plain, white walls with a picture of the prophet Zoroaster. We were not allowed into the room where the fire was burning but from behind a glass wall, we were able to see the flames rising from the large bronze, pedestalled caldron.

'Only the priests who tend the fire are allowed inside. Even they must wear fresh white clothes and a mask to cover their mouths so as not to contaminate the fire with their breath.'

'What's that wonderful smell. Is it from the wood they're burning?'

'Indeed it is, Caroline. Almond and apricot,' Aahil replied. 'And the music in the background is the reading of the Holy Book which is also played continuously. The fire is a symbol of purity and cleanliness. The eternal flame is more than 1500 years old, and it has been burning since 470 AD.'

Caroline had wangled her way right to the front standing next to Aahil, 'How is that possible?'

'As I said earlier, though this actual building is less than a hundred years old, the original fire was brought to Yazd seven hundred years ago. It was kept in the house of the priest until the first temple was constructed. Throughout that time, the fire worshipers have been protecting the eternal flame keeping it alight night and day, and it's never been allowed to go out.'

I glanced round for Robert who was skulking at the back as far away from his wife as possible.

When we all filed out of the temple, I stopped to take another photo and found myself next to him as we walked to the small museum next door.

I felt obliged to say something. 'That was fascinating. I've never even heard of Zoroastrians before we came.'

'Me neither.'

'Not when you were in Iran before?'

He turned to me and frowned. 'This is my first time here.'

'Oh, I must have misunderstood. I thought Caroline mentioned you'd spent a lot of time over in this part of the world when you were in business.'

'We had an office in Turkey. But when you're doing these trips, all you see is the airport and the offices of the company you're visiting. Possibly a hotel room nearby. You might get taken to a local restaurant in the evening but there's never the chance to do any real sightseeing.'

I could hardly ask what had put him in the doghouse with Caroline, but it didn't stop me wondering. She had always struck me as a somewhat timid woman, happy to defer to her husband, and her behaviour had come as a bit of a surprise.

CHAPTER 18

Sunday we were off again on our way to Shiraz. The long journey gave me plenty of thinking time. It would have been good to talk over what Aunt Jessica and I had established so far with her but what with her talk – to which I confess I only half-listened because my attention kept wandering back to the Yusef mystery – and the time she spent wandering up and down the coach answering questions, there wasn't much opportunity.

All we had were questions. Who was our mystery Turk, why was he on the trip at all – he was clearly no tourist, and why would anyone want him dead? There was also the question of whether there was any connection between Yusef's death and any of the other members in our party. Aunt Jessica had claimed on numerous occasions that I have an over-active imagination, attributing all sorts of suspicious motives into perfectly innocent actions or comments, but I was firmly convinced that there was something going on between Irene and Mr Kamali, that Robert was hiding something, and that Paula knew a lot more than she was telling. Though what all that had to do with Yusef's death I couldn't begin to fathom.

After lunch we headed for Pasargadae to see the tomb of Cyrus the Great, who we were told was the founder of the Achaemenian dynasty and who established the largest empire that the world had yet seen.

The tomb itself turned out to be less impressive than I'd

expected. Monumental in size admittedly, commanding the whole valley, but architecturally just an enormous, roofed block on the top of a large step pyramid seemingly stuck in the middle of nowhere.

Not surprisingly, after some two and a half thousand years, little of Cyrus's great city survived. It was a relatively short distance to see the remnants of his palace and even they were little more than rock platforms. Our coach wasn't allowed to drive through the complex, and we had to go with an official guide on one of the open trucks. At first, none of the truck drivers appeared to want to take us and Aahil had a job persuading the head man to find someone to act as our driver. Admittedly, it was getting late and most of them seemed more interested in making tracks for home.

First, we were driven to the acropolis on top of the hill at the far end which was the oldest building on the site. There wasn't much to see so, after taking a few photos, we returned to the truck and were driven back to the Apadana Palace built by Cyrus.

Our guide was pretty useless. A parrot might have shown a bit more enthusiasm, but those in our party who were interested in knowing more followed in Aunt Jessica's wake.

I took the opportunity to sidle up to Paula as she was taking photos of some of the engravings on one of the gate posts which seemed to be the only things standing higher than a few feet from the ground.

After a few comments about the quality of the carvings, I said, 'You know what you were saying the other day about Yusef being a drug smuggler…'

'I didn't say that exactly,' she protested. 'I just thought he seemed a bit odd. Not like a normal tourist at all.'

'I agree. He certainly kept himself to himself.'

She nodded. 'Apart from Barbara who struck up a conversation with him at lunch, the only other person I noticed him talking to was Robert. They were talking for several minutes in the lobby just before we left for the Royal Treasury.'

'Really? You didn't happen to hear what they were talking about?'

'No idea.' She looked at me suspiciously. 'Why do you ask?'

I shrugged. 'No reason. I just wondered.'

Best to change the subject. 'By the way, talking of drugs, I looked up that story you mentioned about the Shah's sister being arrested at some airport for heroin smuggling. From what I read, I had the impression that it was the CIA who got her off, but I wondered how they managed it. I presume they blamed it on someone else, poor sap.'

She laughed. 'I wouldn't get too upset on their behalf. I expect he was very well paid for the years he spent in the slammer.'

'But even so.'

'I don't know about Iran, but I know for a fact that in other Middle Eastern countries, whenever the king's relatives ended up on the wrong side of the law for whatever reason, which they frequently did, some loyal subject would be ready to take the rap for a what was for them a small fortune and a new identity somewhere a long way from home. Given the antics of the Shah's family, it's odds-on it happened quite often.'

My mind was beginning to work overtime but before we could discuss it further, our guide was calling us all together. Paula and I were among the last to arrive and tempers were already beginning to get frayed. The guide was insistent that we get back, but the palace site was extensive, and we'd only seen a small part of it. In the end, a compromise was agreed. The truck would go back but anyone who wished to stay on with Aunt Jessica would walk back when they'd seen the rest of the site. It was quite a hike to get back to our coach, but everyone was so incensed by his attitude that no one opted to drive back with him.

'He's just lost any chance of a tip,' muttered Paula. 'Given that tips are probably his main source of income, he's not a happy bunny.'

'That's what you get when you call Aunt Jessica's bluff.'

It was already dark by the time we reached our hotel – another palace-like affair with a spacious atrium with plush red velvet chairs with gold painted woodwork arranged in small separate open side rooms at the side of a broad marble-floored corridor complete with chandeliers.

Aunt Jessica and I each had a large twin room with queen-sized beds and every mod con. We were due to eat together in the hotel restaurant and there was little time for anything more than a quick shower and change of clothes before dinner.

'You were very quiet this evening. Something up?' Aunt Jessica asked as we rode back up to our rooms in the crowded lift.

I shook my head. 'Bit tired that's all.'

'Me too,' said Mary who was squeezed next to us. 'It never ceases to amaze me how sitting on a coach all day seems to take it out of you just as much as being on your feet all day.'

We had to wait till we reached Aunt Jessica's room that I was able to tell her about Paula seeing Robert talking with Yusef. She didn't look impressed.

'So what? Why shouldn't they be talking?'

'He didn't seem to want to talk to anyone one else.'

'I think you're seeing all sorts of conspiracy theories where none exist,' she said with an indulgent smile. 'Admittedly, Yusef kept himself to himself in the short time we knew him, but there might be all sorts of reasons – he was tired after the long journey, or he was shy. We hardly spent more than three or four hours in the man's company. Given time, he'd probably have opened up to us all.'

'But…'

'Would you have become so hot under the collar if he'd have talked to anyone other than Robert? You seem to have it in for the man.'

She may have had a point, but I wasn't convinced.

'Oh, by the way, I had a text message from my friend at the British Museum. His Iranian colleague confirmed the language Yusef scribbled in his itinerary booklet was Farsi.'

'Yes!' I punched the air. 'I knew it. I told you he was speaking Farsi to the security guard at the bank in Tehran. What did he write?'

'Nothing useful. He sent the translations, but they aren't going to help us any.'

'That's a bummer! I felt certain we'd learn something.'

CHAPTER 19

There was an excited buzz in the air as everyone gathered ready for our departure.

Barbara clapped her hands. 'Persepolis today! This is why I booked the tour.'

'I doubt you're alone. It's always the highlight for everyone who comes.' Aunt Jessica ushered her and the rest of the party to follow Aahil out to the coach.

It was an hour's drive out to the site. The only thing to stare at was virtually featureless desert but nothing could curb my enthusiasm.

'For somewhere seemingly built out in the middle of nowhere, I expected us to be travelling on a simple desert track, but this is one of the best roads we've been on other than the main highways.'

Beside me, Aunt Jessica had taken out her notes and continued to look them over. I wasn't even sure she'd heard me until she said, 'That's because it's part of the last Shah's great fiasco.'

'Oh?'

She turned and smiled. 'You've heard about the party in the desert?'

'Vaguely. Some sort of over-the-top celebration to mark the founding of the Persian Empire, wasn't it?'

'That's one way of putting it. Figures vary according to the sources but even the lowest estimate puts the cost over a hundred million even back in 1971.'

I gave a low whistle.

'He built this road to link the brand-new airport he built in Shiraz to Persepolis for the great event. I expect Aahil will tell everyone more about it when we get there.'

She buried her nose back in her notes and I carried on looking out of the window.

When we arrived, Aahil gave us an introductory spiel before we left the coach.

'The earliest remains date back to 515 BC at the time of Cyrus, whose tomb you saw yesterday. It was intended as the site where he and his descendants came to celebrate the Persian New Year. The actual Palace was built by the next ruler, his son-in-law and distant cousin Darius the Great who not only increased the size of the kingdom but made it the most efficiently ruled empire the ancient world had ever seen. He conceived Persepolis not as his permanent palace but more the spiritual hub of the empire, and it became one of the grandest and most important palaces in the empire. It was here that he received tribute from all the foreign delegations, and nearby is the necropolis where the bodies of all the kings were laid to rest for the next two hundred years until the last Achaemenian king, Darius III was defeated by Alexander the Great who, as I'm sure you all know, burnt the city to the ground.'

We all trooped off the coach. I'm not sure quite what I was expecting. The pictures in Aunt Jessica's PowerPoint presentations had shown impressive carved reliefs but what faced us was a blank high wall that stretched so far in both directions it was difficult to see where it ended. Presumably the vast complex of buildings that Aunt Jessica had talked about lay beyond but there was no gateway through, only a monumental double staircase that rose majestically from the barren plain to what appeared to be a terrace at the top.

'This is probably the best place to take a photo of the Grand Staircase,' Aahil announced. 'Take your time making your way up. There's no hurry. There may be a great many steps, a hundred and ten if you are counting, but they are very shallow. Just imagine you are in the retinue of one of the foreign delegates following the dignitaries on their horses processing up with gifts to present to the King of Kings at the Spring Festival. I can't promise I'll announce your arrival with a trumpet blast when you get to the top as happened back then, but I will be waiting to lead you to the Gate of Nations.'

I stayed behind as I wanted to take more shots, not only of the staircase, but along the length of the whole wall which seemed to stretch endlessly into the distance. Inevitably, I ended up being one of the last to reach the top.

In front of the Gate of Nations was a stall with virtual reality headsets and several of our party had already hired some.

I noticed Aunt Jessica hadn't bothered. 'Is it worth it?'

'As you've never been before, I'd recommend it.'

She was right. The enormous, winged bulls carved on the bottom of pillars either side of the gate were impressive even before I put on the headset but seeing them in full colour with the towering, covered passage beyond was like stepping into another world.

'Wow! I can't get over how tall it was. How on earth did they manage to get up there to build the roof?'

Aunt Jessica laughed. 'Wait till you see the Throne Hall with its hundred pillars and the Audience Hall inside the Apadana Palace.'

We came to the high point of the whole tour – the carvings on the stone staircase up into the palace in the centre of the great complex.

Aahil pointed out each of the delegations from all the dependant states in the empire bringing their gifts to present to the King of Kings. 'We can identify each group from the gifts they are bringing and their clothes, particularly their headgear. See here the Persians with the basket headdresses and Medes in their round caps?'

It was a photographer's paradise. I was so busy snapping away that when I looked up, Aahil and the majority of the group had already started up the steps.

After we'd come out of the small museum in what had once been the Queen's Palace at the back of the complex, we were free to explore the rest of the complex on our own.

I turned to Aunt Jessica. 'What do you fancy looking at?'

'Your choice, sweetie.'

'Didn't Aahil say something about the Palace of Xerxes?'

'That's over there, but apart from a few burnt walls there's not a lot to see. It's where the fire started that destroyed the city.'

'So much for the great hero! Not content with looting the world's richest city, Alexander the Great decided to burn it to the ground. Hardly a noble gesture.'

'Well, accounts differ about what exactly happened. The conventional story may be that once he'd conquered Darius III, he symbolically destroyed the Persian empire by razing its capital to the ground, but some scholars think he may not have been the one who gave the order. Alexander was a Macedonian and supposedly a great admirer of Darius I whom he was keen to emulate. Some authorities claim that it was Alexander's Athenian mercenaries who wanted vengeance because Darius's son Xerxes had destroyed Athens by fire a hundred and fifty years earlier. They took the torches from their stands and set light to the curtains which quickly shot up and destroyed the cedarwood roof. The fire spread through the whole complex in minutes.'

'Seems a long time to hold a grudge.'

Aunt Jessica grinned. 'That's the Greeks for you.'

'If it's all the same to you, I might just pop over and take a couple of shots if only to remind me of that story.'

'No problem. I'll wait for you in the square over there.'

I was gone for rather longer than I intended, and Aunt Jessica looked none too pleased when I returned.

'Sorry about that. I was talking with Aahil.'

'So I saw.' She pursed her lips. 'I've told you before, Harry. You really need to be more circumspect. You're making your interest in our attractive young guide a little too obvious.'

'We were only chatting.' I tried to sound blasé.

'Maybe, but you need to keep a bit more distance. You had your hand on his shoulder just now.'

'It was just a friendly gesture.'

The look she gave me spoke volumes. I was about to storm off, but she seized my arm and held on tightly.

'Don't you understand? It's Aahil's life you're putting in danger. Homosexuality is forbidden in Islamic law. He could be executed or forced to undertake gender reassignment surgery which would result in him being cast out from his family and left without any rights. The only job opportunity he'd have would be as a prostitute.'

'But, as far as I know, Aahil's not gay.'

'That's beside the point. There only has to be a hint of suspicion. SAVAK may have been abolished when the Arab revolution took over but with the ayatollahs firmly in charge, religious laws are strictly enforced. You yourself said that Ali for one has been keeping his beady eye on the two of you.'

'But…' The memory of Paula's pointed comments when we were together on the roof at Rayen came flooding back. If she'd noticed how much time I was spending with Aahil, she probably wasn't the only one.

It made me realise just how selfish I'd been. I enjoyed his company, but I'd given little thought about what the consequences of our friendly chats might be for him.

I sank down on the bench. 'Okay. Point taken.'

Before we all went back to the coach, Aahil led us to the edge of the terrace looking out over the valley spread before us and as Aunt Jessica had promised, he told us about the party in the desert and its eyewatering costs.

'To mark the 2,500-year celebration of the Persian empire, the Shah decided to put on this four-day event here in front of Darius the Great's palace and invited all the world's leaders to witness it. It was the world's most expensive party. He was determined show that Persia could be an important player on the world stage.'

'A modern-day King of Kings, eh?' said Helen.

'Exactly. He spared no expense. Fountains and water features were laid out and thousands of trees and plants were imported to line the pathways between the tents. Flocks of exotic birds were imported which all died off in weeks because they couldn't cope with the climate.'

'How cruel,' protested Mary.

'It must have created work for the ordinary people though, putting on all that spectacle,' Barbara suggested.

'Not at all. The finest foreign architects were brought in to design the complex, and top designers in furniture, textiles, artwork, ceramics and so on were employed from all over Europe. Even the chefs came from top French restaurants and all the food was imported.'

Everyone was still talking about it as we made our way back down the Grand Staircase.

'I saw this American video just before we came out,' said Paula who was walking beside me. 'The guest list read like the who's who of the world leaders with royalty, presidents of state, governors and party chairmen.'

'Including our queen?'

'No, but Prince Phillip and Princess Anne were there as her representatives.'

'I wonder what they thought about living in a tent. I can't quite picture them nipping out to the toilet block in the middle of the night.'

'Stop winding me up,' she said, stopping in her tracks, holding up those who were following us. 'Do you want to hear the rest or not?'

'Of course! It's fascinating.' We continued walking down the steps side-by-side.

'The apartments were more luxurious than any hotel room. Each one even had its own fully staffed kitchen. There were hairdressers, makeup salons all staffed by top French stylists.'

'So what did they all do when they arrived? They didn't just come for a state banquet, I presume.'

'In the morning there was a re-enactment parade to show the 2,500 years of history of the Persian Empire. At night they put on a *Son et Lumiere* production ending with a firework display.'

'You've certainly done your homework.'

She laughed. 'I like to find out as much as I can about a place I'm going to before a visit. Helps me to appreciate the holiday.'

CHAPTER 20

Aunt Jessica and I came down for dinner to find the doors to the dining-room were still closed. Through the glass doors we could see the staff still laying up tables.

'Looks as though they're going to be a while yet. We could go and sit over there.' I pointed to a padded chest under the stairs.

It wasn't long before Helen and Phil came down. There was nowhere else to sit. I stood up and offered my seat to Helen, but she refused, and the couple went to stand by the door. Not long after, we heard footsteps on the floor above and then a mobile rang.

'Hello,' answered a female voice.

Suddenly there was a cry and the sound of someone tumbling down the stairs. Irene lay sprawled at the bottom.

My heart in my mouth, I rushed over in Aunt Jessica's wake to help. I looked down at the still body. My blood ran cold, and I had a momentary flash of déjà vu seeing her lying there. But then her eyes began to flicker open. She was alive.

'Don't try and get up,' commanded Aunt Jessica putting a hand on her shoulder to restrain her.

The sound of the commotion brought two staff running from the dining room and within seconds there was quite a crowd.

I stood back. The poor woman had enough people fussing over her without me. I was aware of a faint squeaky noise. As I bent down, the tinny shrieking voice became clearer. I realised it was from a mobile phone. I spotted it half-hidden under one of the feet of the chest I'd been sitting on. It must have fallen through the banister rails as she fell. I picked it up.

'Cherie, Cherie!'

'Hello?' I answered.

'Who is that? What has happened to Mrs Hoover?'

'I'm afraid she's had an accident. She's just taken a tumble down the stairs.'

'How is she?'

When I didn't answer straightaway, the voice became even more agitated and repeated the question.

'I'm not sure. I don't think she's broken anything.'

I had no idea if that was true, but I had to say something. The man sounded on the verge of hysteria.

'Can I get her to ring you back later?' I hastened to reassure him. 'Who shall I say was calling?'

The phone went dead.

There was no way I could push through the throng to return it. In any case, at this moment she was hardly in a fit state to ring back. I slipped the phone into my pocket.

The manager arrived with the hotel's first aid responder, and he began instructing his staff to usher everyone else away to allow them to see to Irene. The restaurant was opened so most of the crowd disappeared inside. Phil and I hovered just inside the door, waiting for Aunt Jessica and Helen who were still talking to Irene.

'Irene's sitting up. I think she's going to be alright,' I said.

We watched as she was helped to her feet, supported by the two women. A minute or two later the manager led the small party slowly towards a door just beyond the stairs and into a room where Irene could recover away from the gaze of those arriving for dinner.

Phil and I went to find the table our party had been allocated. Robert, Caroline and Barbara were already there and were keen to find out what had happened.

The last to join us were Mary and Gordon.

'Mary was looking out of our bedroom window just now and saw an ambulance arriving. Anyone know who it's for?'

We were already halfway through the meal before Helen and Aunt Jessica arrived.

'Where's Irene? She is alright, isn't she?'

'She's going to be fine. They've taken to hospital just to make sure,' Aunt Jessica explained.

She put up a hand to stop the barrage of questions. 'She hasn't broken anything, thank goodness. Very bruised and still a bit shaky but she banged her head when she fell. Because she may have lost consciousness for a few seconds, the paramedics insisted they take her in for a scan despite her protests. I'm not sure just how much of what she said to the paramedic, the manager actually translated. I rather gained the impression that he was the one who was pressing for her to go to the hospital. Probably to ensure there was no comeback on the hotel.'

'Has anyone told Aahil?' asked Barbara. 'None of us have seen him since we first arrived back to the hotel.'

'I insisted that Irene shouldn't go on her own, but when I offered to go with her, the manager said it would be best if Aahil accompanied her. It makes sense. They probably have someone who speaks good English at the hospital, but if there were any problems, he would be able to explain.'

The group broke up early. It had been another long day, and we'd spent most of it on our feet visiting one site after another. After lunch we'd gone on to look at some ancient tombs carved into the hillside not far from Persepolis itself.

'I know what you told the others, but do you really think she'll be back with us tomorrow?' I asked Aunt Jessica as we walked up to our rooms.

'Oh yes. They might decide to keep her in overnight, but Irene is a very strong-minded woman and if there's no serious damage, she'll discharge herself anyway.'

'Did she say what happened? I noticed she said something to you when she came round, and both of you looked back up the stairs. You were frowning.'

We'd reached our rooms and she beckoned me into hers.

'That's what I wanted to tell you. The first thing she said was that someone pushed her. I looked up but, there was no one there.'

'You think she imagined it?'

Aunt Jessica frowned then shook her head. 'She seemed very certain at the time but when the manager suggested she must have tripped she didn't correct him. In fact, she never mentioned it again. Not in my hearing any way.'

'Perhaps she *was* distracted by the phone call and still a bit confused when she came round again.'

'It's possible, I suppose.'

'That reminds me. I still have her phone in my pocket. It was rather odd actually. When I picked it up, it was a man's voice. He was screaming her name, wanting to know what had happened. When I asked who it was, the phone went dead.'

She pulled a face.

'The thing is he called her Cherie. Do you think she's using a false name?'

'Could be *Chérie* as in sweetheart?' she suggested.

'A boyfriend!'

'And why not, for heaven's sake?'

'That's not what I meant,' I lied, and desperately tried to backpaddle. 'I was going to say he had a foreign accent. I don't think the call came from England.'

'Well let's find out. See who her last call came from.'

I took out Irene's phone and clicked through. 'It just says Hossein. There's no surname.'

'Let's see.' I passed it over.

'You can't do that.' I protested.

The phone began to ring but she switched it off before it rang through.

'I only wanted to see the number.' There was a decidedly smug look on her face. 'As I thought. I recognise that number. It's our Mr Kamali at the Palace hotel. I noticed how friendly those two were when we were there. They may have met when he was a student at The London School of Economics.'

'So he's an old flame. She certainly kept that quiet.'

CHAPTER 21

The departure for our first visit of the day wasn't until nine-thirty but almost all the party turned up soon after breakfast was served at seven. Presumably for the same reason that Aunt Jessica and I decided to forgo a lie-in.

'Any news about Irene?'

'Helen's gone to the reception desk to ask,' said Phil.

I left Aunt Jessica nattering with the others while I went to inspect the cold buffet. I filled my plate with bread, pomegranate sections, dates and something labelled "toot" that looked like giant mulberries.

'You'll get fat eating all those dates,' said Aunt Jessica when I put my plate on the table. 'They're full of sugar.'

'I know but I can't resist them. They are far juicier than anything we get back home. Have you noticed how much better the bread is in this hotel?'

Helen was back before I'd had a chance to get a coffee, but I could tell from her shaking head that there was no news.

I was trying to decide whether or not to fetch something from the hot counter – I'd made a bit of a pig of myself with the bread and fruit – when Aahil arrived, full of smiles.

'I've just been on the phone to the hospital. The doctor has given permission for Irene to leave, and they are finalising the paperwork right now. I'm going to grab a quick bite and then head over to collect her.'

'Does that mean she will be able to come out with us

today?'

'Let me put it like this, Hassan's agreed to drive me over there in the coach so none of us are leaving until we all come back.'

Irene was all smiles when she appeared in the lobby as we gathered for the morning trip. Apart from a nasty bruise on her right cheekbone, half-hidden under the folds of her scarf, she looked her previous perky self.

'I've an enormous bruise on my shoulder, and I managed to skin my elbow plus my hip's still a bit sore, but other than that, I'm fine. They've sent me back with a whole box of painkillers if I need them.

'You were lucky not to have broken anything,' said Helen. 'You gave us all a nasty fright.'

'Surely you're not thinking of coming with us? You need to take it easy today,' admonished Mary.

'I'm perfectly all right. It was only a fall. Apart from a few cuts and bruises, no damage done. Why they insisted on carting me off to hospital I've no idea. I've no intention of sitting around in the hotel all day. Why should I miss out on all the fun? Shiraz is said to be a beautiful city and I don't intend to miss any of it.'

'Good on ya, girl,' I said.

We all piled into the coach.

'You have to give her credit,' I said to Aunt Jessica once we'd sat down. 'Whatever she may say, it was a nasty tumble.'

'True, but she has a point. And the good thing about a city tour like today is that she can pace herself. If things get too tough, she can skip the visit and stay in the coach. If the worst comes to the worst, she can get a taxi back to the hotel.'

Our first visit was to the Pink Mosque famous for its stained-glass windows. The outside wall of the prayer hall was a series of arches filled with solid floor-to-ceiling stained-glass windows. The rays of the early morning sunlight picked up the blues, yellows, greens and oranges as they shone through the geometric panes almost obliterated the designs in the predominantly deep red carpets. As we walked the length of the hall, the effects of the shimmering patterns from the changing angles were stunning.

'I bet you're pleased you didn't miss this, aren't you?' I said to Irene.

'It's quite breath-taking. I'm not sure my photos do it justice. I've been trying to get the effect of the light on the carpet but it's not easy.'

'True, but whenever you look at it in the years to come, it will be enough to remind you of the sense of awe and wonder that you're feeling right at this moment.'

She turned at looked at me. Her face broke into a blissful smile. 'You're right, Harry. I shall treasure this moment. Thank you, young man.'

In complete contrast, our next stop was at a big garden with a palace in the centre.

'Narenjestan Qavan is one of the most famous gardens in Iran. Its name means "the smell of bitter orange blossoms", and you won't be surprised to find that the gardens are full of orange trees. It was founded in the nineteenth century…'

As Aahil continued with his spiel I moved to take photos of the front of the building while all the others were still gathered round him. Inside we found more stained-glass windows and every surface, walls and ceilings was covered in intricate designs and artwork. In one room I discovered a none too happy-looking Gordon Edwards.

'Something wrong?'

'I think I'm going to have to make some time to go through all my photos and delete the rubbish ones. I bought a couple of extra memory cards for this trip, but at this rate, I'm not going to make it to the end of the holiday unless I can find somewhere to buy another one.'

'I brought my laptop, so I've already downloaded quite a few, but I agree it takes time. I don't like to think how many I took at Persepolis yesterday and every room in this place is a treasure trove.'

He chuckled. 'I saw you lying on the floor in the room covered in mirror mosaics to get a shot at the ceiling. Still, I suppose it's so much easier with digital photography. You can click away to your heart's content. You're too young to remember, but when I was your age, back when we were taking prints and transparencies, we had to ration how many photos we could take. When Mary and I went to China back in 2000, I took fourteen rolls of film with me but when we returned home, I realised I must have lost one somewhere. And it cost a bomb to have them all processed. That's when I decided to invest in a digital camera.'

'Sounds as if you're well-travelled.'

'This is our third trip this year,' he admitted a little sheepishly. 'When you get to our age, you never know what the future holds so we take the opportunity to visit all the places on our bucket list while we're still able to do so.'

'And why not! So have you been to this part of the world before?'

'We love Turkey, which is next door of course. We've been there three times. We were in Cappadocia a couple of years ago. At the end of March, we took a cruise that started in the Holy Land, through the Suez Canal to Oman and ended up in Mumbai.'

Interesting that he'd admitted to being in the area. Though I couldn't quite see the amiable Gordon and Mary as possible suspects in any conspiracy concerning Yusef's death.

When we came out of the palace, we were free to explore the gardens by ourselves. It was the first opportunity I'd had to talk to Aunt Jessica.

'I noticed you talking with Irene earlier. Did she say any more about being pushed?'

'The subject didn't come up and I decided not to press her.'

'If she was pushed, it's probably not a good idea for her to wander off on her own.'

'Exactly. I was about to suggest she walk with us, but she mentioned that she and Barbara had arranged to take a short walk before seeing if there was somewhere they could get a cup of coffee.'

Like most traditional Persian gardens, in front of the house was a long narrow stretch of water with flower borders and ornamental trees – in this case, mainly orange trees – either side of the path. We walked down one side, I took a few photos of the distant house from the bottom, and we walked back up the other side.

'I think I'll use the facilities before we get back on the coach,' said Aunt Jessica.

'Good idea.'

As usual, I was outside again long before her. Not wanting to wait immediately outside the low bunker-like building half-hidden down a narrow pathway between the trees, I walked back up to the open gardens. Quite by chance, I spotted Irene sitting on a stone bench in the formal rose garden. It was too good an opportunity to miss. I'd been trying to get her on her own all morning.

Her mobile was still in my pocket. I'd waited to return it as there were a few questions I wanted to ask but didn't want to discuss it with anyone else in earshot.

You'd think I'd handed her the crown jewels.

'I thought I'd lost it altogether. Thank you so much.' She clutched it to her chest. 'I didn't realise it was missing until I was in the hospital and wanted to make a call. I must have dropped it when I fell. I asked at reception, but they said no one had handed it in.'

'Sorry. I should have told them I'd found it. It was under

the staircase. I thought it best to look after it until you came back.'

'I have it now, that's the main thing.'

'Perhaps you should phone back the friend you were speaking to before you fell.'

'I have already. When I realised, I no longer had my mobile, I asked a nurse to get me a public phone.'

'Mr Kamali was worried about you.'

'You spoke to him?'

'That's how I found your phone. I heard a voice calling.'

'You told him what happened?'

I nodded.

'He didn't mention it.'

'How long have you known him?'

The frown had turned into a broad smile. 'We were students together at university a long time ago.'

'Old boyfriend, was he?'

'Oh no,' she gave deep hearty chuckle. 'To be honest I didn't know him that well. He was more a friend of a friend. Once I'd dropped out of the course I was doing, we never saw each other again.'

'Really?'

As I hoped, she looked straight at me.

'He called you *chérie*.'

She burst out laughing. 'Not *chérie*. Sheri. It was what all my mates called me from when I started school. My maiden name was Sheringham. And to be honest, back then I never liked the name Irene. It was old-fashioned even then. I think poor Hossein was surprised when I walked into his hotel. Neither of us recognised each other at first. We've both changed quite a bit in forty years. He's lost his hair and grown a moustache and we've both put on a good few pounds!'

'But you never let on.'

'It wasn't a secret, but you have to admit, after that dreadful accident there were other things on everyone's mind. Once we'd left Tehran, it didn't seem relevant.'

'I suppose not.'

I could see Aunt Jessica emerging from the path and gave her a wave.

'Irene's just been telling me that she and Mr Kamali were students together back in London. Small world, isn't it?'

'Indeed, it is.'

Irene looked at her watch. 'I think it's time I started getting back. I don't want to be the last to arrive and I'd rather not rush.'

'We'll come with you.'

Aunt Jessica was surprisingly quiet on the coach journey to our next visit. Not that she's prone to chat away endlessly in any case, but I could tell something was up.

'Penny for them.'

'What?'

'Anything wrong?'

'No. Just trying to work something out, that's all.'

'I rather gathered that. Shpill the beans, pardner,' I said doing my best Humphry Bogart impression.

'Grow up, Harry.'

She only called me by my given name when she was annoyed with me, so I decided it was best to drop the subject. At least for now.

CHAPTER 22

Our next stop was another mosque, but this was completely different again because all the women were made to cover themselves completely before they could go inside. Instead of the traditional black chadors, they were given loose robes of pale flowery material to wrap over their heads and bodies so that only their face peeped out. Inevitably, this caused a great deal of hilarity and we men spent some time taking photos of them.

From there, the coach took us to the centre of town and dropped us off on the edge of a large pedestrian square.

Aahil gathered us together. 'From here we will walk to the bazaar.'

In front of us was a large fortress-like building with solid high brick walls and round towers at each corner.

'Is that another of those places they built for the traders and their caravans to stop?' asked Mary.

'It's served a great many functions over the years, but it was never a caravanserai.' Aahil frowned and shook his head. 'It was built as a royal residence in the eighteenth century by Karim Khan when he decided to make Shiraz his capital.'

'With all those bands of geometric brickwork, the towers are very attractive.'

'If you want the best angle to take a photo, see that statue of a tourist with a camera over on the corner? You might like to go and stand next to him.'

Once we'd all had a chance to take our pictures, Aahil

led us slowly past the tower towards the bazaar.

'That tower looks as if it might fall over any minute,' said Robert.'

'And there's a huge crack in the wall. That must be dangerous,' added his wife.

'Not anymore,' Aahil cut in quickly. 'Recently more work has been done to ensure it does not move any further. You remember I said this building has been used for many things? For thirty years it was used as a prison and that tower was converted into the toilet block for all the inmates. As time went on, the sewage system gradually washed away the soil beneath and about thirty years ago it began to lean. It wasn't possible to right it again, but it has been made safe.'

As we neared the bazaar, numerous small shops began to line the streets. As everyone gathered around Aahil as he identified the various dried herbs heaped up in attractive blue bowls on the open pavement table, I took the opportunity to have a quiet word with Aunt Jessica.

'Sorry if I was being an idiot earlier.'

'I'm the one who should apologise. I didn't mean to snap, but something's been worrying me.'

'Aunt Maud? You haven't had any news?'

'No nothing like that. Maud is as tough as old boots. She'll outlast all us Hamilton sisters. Besides, your mother would phone if she suddenly took a turn for the worse.'

'In that case, what is the problem?'

'I was thinking about Irene. It's that comment she made when she came round after that fall.'

'About being pushed?'

'It wasn't so much as what she said as the sheer terror on her face when she looked back up the stairs.'

'You think she saw who it was?'

'That's one of the things I've been thinking about, but I don't believe so. I looked up to see what was frightening her and there was no one there. At least not by then.'

'Even if there was someone, wouldn't they have had

time to disappear while she was unconscious?'

'She was only out for a few seconds, half a minute at most. If it was accidental – Irene stopped suddenly, and someone crashed into her – then surely, they would have raced down the stairs to see how she was?'

'But you're saying, if someone deliberately pushed her, they would have disappeared before anyone saw them.'

'Exactly.'

'But who would want to hurt Irene of all people? She could have died.'

Aunt Jessica stated the obvious. 'Until we know the reason why, we can't even begin to speculate who.'

Once we left the wide, open road and went through the main gate into the enclosed bazaar, the atmosphere was very different. Here the passageway was narrow and crowded. It was like stepping into another world. I stood still for a moment or two, drinking in the noisy call of the stallholders and the bargaining shoppers; the wonderful smells of spices, fresh fruit, leather goods even the distinct aroma coming from the lamb's wool tassels; and the sheer glorious colours of shimmering fabrics hanging from the top of the walls, of patterned carpets, multi-coloured slippers and gleaming copper bowls.

Though Aahil walked slowly identifying the various herbs, spices and sweetmeats on display, it wasn't long before our little party began to separate. Mary was the first to dive off to haggle with a shop keeper, but others soon followed suit while several people lingered to take photos.

'I don't think you need worry about Irene,' said Aunt Jessica. 'She and Barbara have teamed up and so far, they seem to be staying close to Aahil. I doubt she'll come to any harm. Besides, if she spots you trying to dog her footsteps all the time, you'll make her think you're the one up to no good.'

I nodded. 'You have a point. Any ideas about what I can get as presents to take back? There were some beautiful scarves back there, but I gave them all scarves when we went to Morocco.'

We all met up again when we reached the caravanserai in the centre of the bazaar. Inside, around the large central square complete with large pond and orange trees were more small shops but these were all selling more expensive craft items.

'These blue vases are very pretty,' I said.

We'd stopped to look in a window crammed with elaborately shaped blue patterned bowls, plates, lidded pots and vases.

'If you're thinking of any of those as presents, I should warn you each one is individually made in copper and the enamel work on top takes weeks of work before they're fired, which means they don't come cheap.'

In the end, I settled on a small painted box for my mother. It was carved camel bone and consequently pretty pricey. I decided to save it for her Christmas present and find something else for her and my aunts as holiday gifts somewhere else.

Just off the main square was a café. Helen and Phil were sitting at one of the tables outside.

'May we join you?'

'Please do.' Helen moved a couple of bags of shopping from one of the chairs.

As we sat down, I could see Aunt Jessica scanning the tables inside. She said nothing but I could tell from her expression that she was relieved to see Irene sitting with Barbara at a small table near the counter.

'Do the waiters come out or do we order inside?' I asked.

'Not sure. We ordered inside.'

'In that case I'll go in. What would you like?'

'A coffee will be fine.'

'Nothing to eat?'

'Not for me.'

As I made my way inside, my brain was working overtime. If I'd had any doubts about the seriousness of the situation before, Aunt Jessica's obvious concern convinced me. I may be given to flights of fancy, but Aunt Jessica always kept her feet firmly on the ground. There may not have been any conclusive proof that Yusef's death was not an accident or that Irene had been deliberately pushed down the stairs, but the coincidence of two highly suspicious events occurring within days of one another was becoming harder to accept.

I waved at Barbara as I caught her eye on my way to the counter and she waved back. I spotted a gooey chocolate cake in the cabinet on the counter.

'Couldn't resist the temptation,' I said as I laid the plate on the table. 'I've brought two forks, but I can go back and get one for you too, if you fancy it?'

'It's all yours.' Aunt Jessica smiled. At least she seemed considerably more relaxed now she knew Irene was safe. Though quite what harm could come to the woman in such a busy place I couldn't quite fathom.

'They'll bring the coffees when they're ready.'

I sat down and turned my attention to Helen. 'I see you've been shopping again. I spotted you inside that copper shop earlier looking at the cooking pots. Is that what's in the big bag? It looks heavy.'

'Mary bought quite a fancy one in Yazd which I admired. This is quite plain. More functional than the ones to hang on the wall or put on a shelf.'

'I keep telling her,' said Gordon, 'It's not the weight of all these things she keeps buying that we have to worry about, it's how we're going to get them home. You're only allowed so much hand luggage on the plane going home.'

'I'll fill it with the dirty washing and squeeze it in the bottom of the case. And both cases were well under the limit when we came out.'

'Maybe, but all those picture books you keep buying are

heavy.' Phil may have had a smile on his face as he spoke, but I sensed a growing frustration at her refusal to appreciate a warning he'd probably already given her several times previously.

After we'd left the café, we still had half an hour to kill before we were due to meet up again with Aahil to go back to the coach.

'Unless you want to continue looking round the shops, I'd quite like to get a few more photos of the architecture of this place. The people of Shiraz obviously treated their travelling merchants from the East as highly-valued guests to put them up in such magnificent quarters.'

'Fine by me.'

'What I can't get over is how the patterns in the brickwork of those domed ceilings is all so different, not to mention that blue tilework on the arches. Every one of them throughout the whole complex is unique.'

After ten minutes of trailing after me, I suggested Aunt Jessica go back to the central square. There were benches around the square pond where she could sit and wait for me.

When I eventually went to join her, she was talking to Irene. I could see that Irene was beginning to droop. Her face was noticeably paler and more lined than at the start of the day. Whatever she might say, that fall was taking its toll. She shifted further along the bench to make room for me to sit down, and gave a sudden cry. She eased her shoulders forward.

'Did you bring those painkillers with you?' said Aunt Jessica.

'There's a packet in my bag.'

'I'll get it.'

Aunt Jessica bent down to retrieve the handbag tucked under the bench. She took out a small white box bearing a hospital label, plus a small bottle of water. After a minute or two, the colour came back to Irene's cheeks, and she relaxed her shoulders.

'Sorry about that. My back's a bit sore.'

'Is that from where he pushed you?'

Irene snapped her head round to look Aunt Jessica in the eye.

'I'm sorry?'

'When I was helping you up after your fall, you said someone had pushed you.'

Irene's eyes narrowed and it was some moments before she shook her head. 'You must have misheard me. Who on earth would want to do such a thing?'

'Exactly. That's what Harry and I have been wondering.'

Irene shook her head. 'I tripped. I was answering a call and didn't pay enough attention.'

Pain or no pain, she struggled to her feet and started to move away from us.

'We were wondering if it had anything to do with the death of Yusef Kaya.'

Irene halted in her tracks, but she didn't look round. Then she continued walking towards the corner where Aahil was standing with a small group of the others.

I went to follow, but Aunt Jessica put out a hand. 'Let her go. She's now aware that we know. When she's had a chance to think it over, she may begin to appreciate we are on her side.'

CHAPTER 23

It had been another packed day but there was no evening lecture before dinner which was probably all to the good. Even if Aunt Jessica had had the energy to give it, I'm not sure that the others would have been up for it. I left Aunt Jessica to rest and went back to my own room to download my photos and look at them on my laptop.

By dinner time everyone appeared back to their normal enthusiastic selves. Irene, who seemed much recovered, was sitting at the far end of the table, giving us a wide berth. Presumably she didn't want to risk Aunt Jessica asking her any more awkward questions.

I left Aunt Jessica discussing the poetry of Harfez, whose tomb had been our last visit of the day, with Phil and Helen, and went to get myself a second helping from the buffet table.

When I sat down again, Aunt Jessica was staring across the room at Irene who was standing just outside the open restaurant doors.

'Something wrong?'

'That's the third time in the last half hour she's tried to make a call and given up.'

'Perhaps whoever she's ringing is busy.'

'The thing is she's looking progressively more anxious.'

I looked across at Irene who now had her mobile clutched to her chest.

'She's trying again,' I said in surprise.

This time, her call was answered. She turned away so we

couldn't read her expression. Two minutes later, she staggered to the nearest chair on the far side of the corridor and sank down, head bowed.

Aunt Jessica was by her side in a flash. I was too far away to hear what she was saying and as I slowly made my way over, Irene's phone dropped to her lap, and she hid her face in her hands.

I hovered in the doorway uncertain whether to join them or not. It was clear my presence wasn't needed. I found a nearby chair and perched. A few moments later, Aunt Jessica turned to look round and when she saw me, beckoned me over.

'Irene's not feeling too great. Will you help me get her to her room?'

Once we were upstairs, Irene sank into one of the armchairs by the window. Aunt Jessica knelt beside her.

'Will you get her a glass of water please, Harry?'

There was a carafe of drinking water and a couple of glasses on a tray on top of the chest of drawers.

By rights, I should probably have left them to it and made myself scarce, but before I reached the door, I decided to perch on the end of the furthest of the two queen-sized beds well out of their eyeline.

'Exactly who has gone missing?' Aunt Jessica's voice was low and reassuring.

'Hossein.'

'Mr Kamali? From the hotel in Tehran.'

'I've been trying to phone him all morning but there's been no answer, so I rang reception. They put out a general call for him. No one in the hotel has seen him since this morning.'

'There's probably a simple explanation.'

A tear ran down Irene's cheek and she wiped it away with the back of her hand. 'Something's happened to him.'

'We don't know that yet.'

'But don't you see, it must be linked to...' She shrank

back into her chair.

'Linked to the attempt to push you down the stairs or to the death of Yusef Kaya?'

Irene stared wide-eyed at Aunt Jessica. 'You know, don't you?'

'Harry and I have worked out a few things, but if you were pushed, why didn't you tell the police?'

Irene shook her head so violently; her scarf collapsed around her shoulders. 'I can't.'

'Why not, for heaven's sake?'

'You don't understand. I can't go to the police.'

'But if Hossein really is missing, the hotel will inform the police and they will be involved anyway.'

Irene buried her face in her hands.

Aunt Jessica reached out a hand. 'We want to help, Irene, but we can't do that unless you tell us exactly what's going on.'

'You don't understand.' Her voice was so soft, I barely heard it. 'What Hossein and I were planning to do wasn't exactly legal.'

'I promise you, we're on your side. You have to trust us.'

After what seemed an age, Irene hung her head and said in a muffled whisper, 'It's a long story.'

'We've plenty of time. Let's start with what you've already told us about you and Hossein Kamali being students together. Was all that true?'

'As far as it went, but I didn't really know him that well back then. I haven't seen him since he returned to Iran after university, but he and I made contact again about four months ago.' More tears glistened on her eyelashes.

Aunt Jessica proffered the box of tissues. Once she'd patted away the dampness and blown her nose, Irene continued, 'Hossein was the best friend of my fiancé. Mahmoud and I were planning to get married after we graduated. The plan was that he would stay in Britain and get a job. There were problems. Like most noble Iranians back then, his parents had arranged a marriage for him into a very wealthy family. Because of the shame it would bring on his family if he didn't go through with it, one of his fellow Iranian students threatened to inform on him to the Shah's secret police and have him arrested if he didn't go back. When Mahmoud went missing, we assumed that's what happened. When he left without even saying goodbye I...,' her voice broke, and she screwed the tissue into a tiny ball. Looking down, she continued in a half whisper, 'I had a nervous breakdown. I dropped out of uni and went back to Northampton to live with my parents.

'And Yusef? How does he fit into all this?'

'His name wasn't Yusef Kaya, and he wasn't Turkish.'

'He was the student who betrayed your fiancé, I take it.'

She nodded. 'His real name was Reza Darbandi. He was also Mahmoud's second cousin. They grew up in the same town.'

'Did you and Hossein arrange to have him killed?'

'Of course not! We only wanted to confront him. Threaten to tell the authorities he was over here on a forged passport unless he told us what happened to Mahmoud. His death was just an unfortunate street accident.'

Aunt Jessica shook her head. 'I don't think so. And neither do you. You may have thought so at the time but after your fall, and now Mr Kamali's disappearance, it's clear all these things must be connected.'

'But how? I don't understand what's going on. What am I going to do?'

She burst into tears. It was obvious Aunt Jessica would get no more out of her tonight. Aunt Jessica took her in her arms until the sobbing began to die down.

'You're exhausted. I think right now it might be best if I help get you to bed. You need a good night's sleep. I'm sure Hossein will be back in the morning, and you've been upsetting yourself over nothing. If he's not, I promise you we'll come up with a plan of action. You're not alone anymore.'

Time for me to make myself scarce. Not that I went far. I hovered in the doorway of my room a few doors further down the corridor. It was ten minutes before Aunt Jessica emerged.

'How is she?'

'A great deal calmer now. She's taken one of her sleeping pills. She doesn't take them regularly but often brings some on holiday in case her sleep patterns get mixed up or the hotel is noisy.'

I glanced at my watch. 'It's just gone nine-thirty. It's a bit early to call it a day. Do you want to go back down again?'

'What do you want to do?'

I realised all the tension had made my throat quite dry. 'I fancy a drink, actually.'

We walked down the staircase and found a quiet spot away from the crowds clustered close to the bar.

There was a harassed-looking waiter doing the rounds taking orders, but there was a large crowd of noisy German tourists all demanding attention and it was clear it would be some time before he reached us. I decided to go straight to the bar. Aunt Jessica was deep in thought when I returned with our drinks.

I'd already drunk half my beer – normally I'm not much of a beer drinker but I was thirsty and the stuff they brew for the tourists in Iran is pretty mild – when I noticed Aunt Jessica had hardly taken more than a sip.

'I wonder what she meant when she said what she and Mr Kamali had planned to do wasn't legal?'

Aunt Jessica slowly shook her head from side to side. 'No idea.'

'But what do you think? Is someone after Irene and Mr Kamali because they arranged for Yusef to be killed or is the same man responsible for all three attacks?'

'Assuming Mr Kamali really is missing.'

'Granted. But why?'

The only answer was a shrug.

'Why do I get this feeling you're not ready to believe

Irene's story?'

'I don't think she's lying. It's just that I don't think she's telling us the full story.'

'She knows who is behind all this, you mean?'

She frowned, then slowly shook her head. 'I'm fairly certain she doesn't. That's what's terrifying her.'

CHAPTER 24

I spent most of the night tossing and turning. There were so many unanswered questions. What was it Irene wasn't telling us? Who had pushed her down the stairs? Why? Where was Hossein? Was he caught up in all this?

Around three in the morning, I woke breathless in a cold sweat from a weird dream in which Irene was some kind of secret agent working undercover on the trail of a heroin trafficker. She and I were creeping along a dark narrow street lit by a single dim streetlight, following a tall man in a hat and a long raincoat. I couldn't see his face, but his walk seemed familiar. I was just about to reach him when two men dressed in black jumped out from a side alley and came for me, the blades of their long scimitars flashing in the lamplight. I turned and ran, my heart pounding.

I don't know if I'd cried out, but my tongue felt as though it was stuck to the roof of my mouth. I staggered to the bathroom and drank three glasses of water straight off.

The nightmare had been so vivid that I took some time to fall asleep again.

Given the choice, Aunt Jessica always preferred to eat at a table next to the window. Whether that was because after a lifetime spent out in the open air on archaeological digs, she preferred to sit in the lightest, most open spot. Or perhaps, it was less noisy or just the best place from which to people-watch, I had no idea. She had once remarked that if it wasn't because she spent so much of her time in the British Museum either researching or giving gallery talks to visitors, she would have chosen to live somewhere in the country within easy access of remote spots where she could enjoy the peace of open spaces whenever she fancied.

The next morning, by the time we arrived downstairs, we really didn't have much choice about where we sat. Half a dozen of our party had beaten us down to breakfast and were all sitting together. With two empty chairs at their table in the centre of the room, we could hardly ignore them.

Apart from a brief coffee stop, we spent most of the morning travelling in the coach on our way to Isfahan.

As I stared out of the window at the passing landscape, try as I might to ignore it, the same question kept coming back to my mind. What if it had been one of our party had pushed Irene down the stairs? I went through every single member of the group trying to dream up a possible motive without success. Despite all my earlier suspicions about her involvement in Yusef's accident, I was forced to admit Irene was a friendly, pleasant individual and as far as I knew, she'd had no bust-ups with anyone.

I even considered Aahil and the two drivers. There was something about Ali that made me uneasy though I couldn't pinpoint exactly what. Perhaps because he thought I was paying too much attention to Aahil. Even so, I couldn't come up with a plausible explanation as to why he might have it in for Irene.

Whether it was because of all those articles I'd been reading on heroin smuggling in Iran, I had a gut feeling it had to be something to do with that. Though how that might involve Irene was a complete mystery.

I felt decidedly bleary-eyed as we went into lunch.

'We keeping you up?' said Paula as I tried to stifle a

yawn.

'Sorry. Age creeping up on me.' I pretended to stagger up the half dozen steps to the narrow terrace hemmed in by tall bushes to where a long table had been laid out for us.

'You poor old man.'

I decided that this was as good a chance I'd get as any to quiz her. Though I had no doubts that she was ruthlessly ambitious and would have no qualms about using people to further her career, I couldn't see her going so far as to injure anyone, let alone Irene. Nonetheless, I had no other suspects so I might as well seize the opportunity now it had presented itself.

'M' lady.' I pretended to do the gentleman thing and pulled one of the ironwork chairs from under the table for her and did a deep bow.

'Why thank you, kind sir. That was a fascinating talk Jessica gave on the coach. I'd never even heard of the Safavids before we came on this trip.'

'Me neither. Though I have to confess, I kept falling asleep so I'm not that much wiser even now.'

'Shame on you!'

It wasn't until we'd finished our main course that I started probing.

'You know what you were saying a couple of days ago about heroin smuggling? The more I think about it, the more I think you might have a point.'

'About Yusef?'

'You know how, when you can't get to sleep, all sorts of silly ideas go round in your head? What if he was connected in some way to some drug racket, do you think someone could have been following him?'

'An undercover agent?' She let out a girlish giggle. 'Well, if they were, they must have been gutted when he was knocked down in a street accident.'

Either she was a damn good actress, or I was barking up the wrong tree.

'It'd make a great story though, wouldn't it?'

'Harry! Much as I would love to be, as I told you before, I am *not* an investigative reporter. I'm an insignificant backroom office researcher occasionally let out to do the rubbish jobs no one else wants.'

'So you said, but I thought most reporters had this hankering to write a great novel. Let's face it, a trip like this one could stimulate all sorts of ideas. And as you've admitted, you do have a great imagination.'

'Exactly the same could be said of you! So, if you're upset I might be going to steal your thunder, don't worry. I assure you that's the last thing on my mind. You go ahead and write your masterpiece. I didn't even do English at A' level. My degree is in Geography and the only thing you can really do with that is teach which I definitely did not want to do. The only job I could get when I first left uni was working unsociable hours for a minimum wage as a waitress in a restaurant. I spent the next five years working as an office manager in a small building firm which was equally boring, but the pay was better. It may not be the most enviable job in the world but, if I play my cards right, my present post could at least give me a chance to move into something better.'

I put my hands up in protest. 'I have trouble writing anything longer than a text message.'

We both laughed. It was time to make our way back to the coach.

We'd been driving for about forty minutes when Aahil announced that there were camels coming up on the left side of the coach.

I picked up my camera and turned to Aunt Jessica. 'Do you mind if I push past and get a photo?'

'Be my guest.'

Even with her leg rest stretched out in front of her, there was more than enough room to get by without disturbing her too much. Luckily, there was no one in the seat opposite. I perched on the edge of the seat, lining up the camera as we approached the small herd.

'They're not wild. They have just been left out here to fend for themselves. If you look at their feet, you can see they've been hobbled so they can't travel any distance,' said Aahil.

I managed to take several decent shots, then twisted back into the seat to check the results. I put my hand in my pocket to retrieve the lens cap. Not a good idea. I managed to catch hold of my handkerchief at the same time, sending loose coins all over the seat. I heard several clatter to the floor.

'Damn.'

Down on my hands and knees scrabbling beneath the seat, I managed to retrieve the half dozen I could see. Though I'd already picked up my pen that had fallen onto the seat, I decided to run the tips of my fingers between the gap between the seat and the backrest. I touched something tucked a good inch or so in.

No coin could have made its own way so far, but my curiosity roused, I persevered.

'Look what I found,' I said to Aunt Jessica once I was back in my seat.

'What is it? A USB stick.'

'Looks like it. Could be someone's using it to download photos. I'll give it to Aahil, and he can use the microphone to ask if anyone's lost theirs.'

She looked thoughtful. 'I doubt it's one of our group. Have you seen anyone sitting there?'

'Only Yusef when we travelled from the airport.'

'And again when the coach dropped us off outside the National Treasury. I suggest we take it back and download the contents before we hand it over.'

'But he wouldn't have had time to take any photos,' I protested.

'Assuming that's what's on it.'

'You think it could be a clue?'

She smiled. 'Unless we take a look, we'll never know.'

CHAPTER 25

After a couple of hours, we stopped again in a small village which, to judge from the degraded high adobe walls, was a remnant of what many years before had been a thriving town. There was a small pottery shop where we watched a short demonstration. To judge from the small parcels that most of the group left with, it appeared I was one of the few not to have bought something. I had scoured the shelves for possible presents but decided the house in Norfolk had more than enough knickknacks without adding more.

Afterwards we went for a walk through the village. Down a small side street, little more than a narrow passageway between badly eroded mud walls, which looked as if it would lead to more ruins, we came to a door in a high wall.

'This is the entrance into what was once a caravanserai. As the town is on the main road from Shiraz to Isfahan, it's being renovated into a hotel for today's travellers. If you wait just a moment, I'll see if they'll let us in to have a look round.'

We didn't have to wait long. Aahil was back within minutes, and we all trooped in after him.

Given that we'd come in through an unimposing door in a blank wall in a narrow street, the inside was impressive covering a vast area. As this wasn't a scheduled visit, we were free to wander about by ourselves although Aunt Jessica did something of an impromptu tour pointing out various features. After a while, I decide to explore the upper sections. I wasn't the only one who bothered to climb the steep steps which appeared to put off nearly everyone else. As I looked down into the central courtyard, I noticed Robert taking photos on the other side.

'Spectacular, isn't it?' I said, when I caught up with him.

He nodded. 'They're making a great job of it. Once the place is up and running it will be magnificent. If ever we come back, we'll have to see if we can stay here.'

'Are you likely to do that? Come back to Iran, I mean.'

'Never say never, but probably not. Caroline has her heart set on Thailand next. There are quite a few places on her bucket list.'

'Iran was your choice then, was it?'

'I was probably the one who suggested it, but once she saw the pictures in all the brochures, she was more than happy.'

'What made you choose this particular tour?'

'The itinerary, I suppose.'

He answered readily enough and didn't seem to find my questions suspicious at all, but I decided it was probably time to drop the subject. If he was the spy in the camp, I was in too perilous a location to give him any excuse to think I might be on to him.

'I think Aahil's beginning to gather everyone together. Perhaps we should go back down and join them.'

It wasn't until we arrived at our next hotel – another sumptuous establishment worthy of the palace of the great Shah Abbas himself after whom the hotel was originally named – that I had the chance to download the info on the USB stick I'd found on the coach.

'Why would anyone want to hide to a photo of well-heeled people sitting around a roulette wheel?' I asked.

'No idea, but that photo certainly wasn't taken anywhere in Iran. It's against the Koran to gamble.' Aunt Jessica gently stroked her chin. 'Click on to the next one.'

There were a couple of pictures shot from a different angle plus two taken at a blackjack table. To judge from the piles of chips stacked in front of each of the players, they were playing for high stakes. Though given the glitter from the obscene amount of diamond jewellery sported by languorous young women in low-cut gowns clinging to the players' arms, what the men stood to lose was probably little more than pin money to them.

The last three showed the same good-looking young Persian man outside the club with a woman on each arm about to get into a limo drawn up at the foot of the entrance steps.

'I can't see Yusef in any of the photos, can you?' I asked.

She shook her head. 'Looking at that car and the hairstyles, I think the original pictures were taken a good few years ago and if I'm not mistaken that's the Grosvenor in Soho. As Irene said people change a good deal over the years but he,' she pointed to the man in the last picture, 'can't be Yusef. Whoever he is, is tall. Almost six-foot.'

'So what was Yusef doing with the pictures? And why did he hide them on the coach?'

We both sat silently for a while.

'Assuming as he claimed, Yusef's room was searched. Do you think that's why he pushed it where no one would think to look? Down the back of his seat on the coach.' I felt triumphant. 'That's why he was here. He was going to blackmail whoever is in those pictures. It has to be!'

'Hold on Harry. Someone else entirely may have lost that stick months ago and over time it's slipped further and further out of reach.'

Trust Aunt Jessica to bring me back to earth with a bump.

She must have seen the expression on my face because she patted me on the shoulder. 'All the same, we need to find out exactly who this young man is, because if you're right, we may have cracked the case. Or, at least, be a good deal closer to the answer.'

'Fine. But how do you propose we identify him?'

'For a start, can you crop the most suitable pictures to show just his face so I can show his portrait around.'

'Sure.'

'We might make a start with Irene. See if she recognises him.'

'Talking of Irene, I don't suppose you've had a chance to wheedle any more out of her today?'

'Not yet. It's been tricky to get to speak to anyone on their own while we've been travelling. Though I did see you and Robert together at the caravanserai. Not grilling him again, were you?'

'I'm convinced he's been to Iran before. He seems to know an awful lot about the country and its customs.'

'You should watch your step. If it turns out that he really is this Mr Big that you seem to have him down as, then you need to be careful what you say. You might be the next one to fall from a great height. And you might not be so lucky.'

CHAPTER 26

Aunt Jessica was due to give another talk before dinner. I'd enjoyed putting together the presentation for this talk because of the wonderful pictures, which was why she'd decided not to give the talk on the coach. It was all about Shah Abbas I – one of the country's most influential rulers and one of my favourite characters. He had made Isfahan his capital and remodelled the city to show the wealth and grandeur of his reign.

Aunt Jessica had stressed when we left the coach, the talks were entirely optional and no one should feel guilty if they wanted to rest, but once again, the whole party turned up. Several had even brought pens to scribble notes on the handouts. Even Irene had decided to come down.

It hadn't been the most taxing of days and she looked more her normal self. When she arrived, I was already sitting at the front ready to jump up and collect the various handout sheets at the appropriate time in the talk. Irene chose a seat at the back. I wondered if that was to put as much distance from Aunt Jessica and me as possible. It wouldn't be true to say that she had avoided us all day, but I had noticed she hadn't looked me in the eye. No doubt she was regretting her emotional outpourings about Mr Kamali on our last night in Shiraz.

During the questions at the end of the talk, I made my way to the back and switched off the projector. The bulb needed time to cool down before the whole thing could be moved, so I hadn't specifically planned on being able to talk to Irene at the end when everyone began to leave. Not that I intended to waste the opportunity.

'It's good to see you looking so much better today.'

'Thank you. Yes. I'm feeling quite my old self again.' She was too polite to ignore me, but she still didn't look me in the eye.

'That's good because, by the looks of things, we're all going to be put through our paces again tomorrow. It's going to be a packed day in Isfahan.'

Aunt Jessica had also lost no time in nipping to the back to join us.

'That was a lovely talk, Jessica. I confess I'd never even heard of Abbas the Great before we came.'

'I don't think many people outside this part of the world have. Talking about hearing about people, have you heard any more about what's happened to Hossein Kamali? I've been thinking about the poor man all day.'

It hadn't been a subtle jump to a leading question but the genuine concern in Aunt Jessica's tone softened any quick withdrawal on Irene's part. Her body tensed only momentarily before her shoulders sagged and she slowly shook her head and sank back down on her chair.

'I tried getting in touch with the hotel again just before I came down. They promised me yesterday that they'd ring me the minute they heard any news but there's been nothing all day.' Her voice was barely above a whisper, and I had to strain to hear her.

Aunt Jessica pulled round a chair to face her and sat down. 'You don't have his home number?'

She shook her head. 'But when the hotel couldn't get an answer, the undermanager sent someone round to check. His wife died some years ago, so they contacted his brother-in-law. He'd not heard from him for over a week.'

I decided to keep my distance. Irene had developed a bond with Aunt Jessica. I continued packing away the equipment with my back to them but made sure I was close enough to hear.

'You've no idea what might have happened?'

'I've been wracking my brain ever since last night.'

'Who else knew the two of you were planning to force Yusef to tell you what happened to your fiancé?'

'No one. He may have told his family he was hoping to get some answers as to what happened to Mahmoud. They'd always been told that he'd been smuggled out of London to America before the secret police came for him, but they never found out exactly where he went. The story went that because SAVAK had spies everywhere, it would be dangerous for him if they tried to contact him, but as soon as it was safe to do so, Mahmoud would get in touch with them.'

'Presumably, that never happened?'

'The family hoped that after the revolution and SAVAK was disbanded, they would hear something, but he never made contact.'

'And there's never been any news?'

Irene shook her head.

'What I don't understand is why you've waited all this time before the pair of you decided to track him down?'

Irene let out a pained sigh. 'Apparently, last year Mahmoud's mother became desperately ill. She needed an operation which the family could not afford but – out of the blue – they were contacted by a leading hospital to say that an anonymous American donor had paid for her treatment.'

'Presumably, they believed that was Mahmoud.' Aunt Jessica frowned. 'But if that was the case, why hadn't he contacted them before?'

'Perhaps they assumed he must have made a new life for himself out in America. All I know is that once his mother was well and home again, the family set about trying to trace this mysterious donor. The hospital couldn't help – the financial arrangements were all done through lawyers – so they started to contact all of Mahmoud's old university friends which was how Hossein came to be involved. He decided that the one person who would know if Mahmoud had managed to evade the secret police back in 1978 was Reza.'

'Is that when the pair of you decided to track him down?'

'Not at all. I didn't know anything about the story. I didn't hear it until a few months ago when Hossein contacted me out of the blue and told me.'

'So what did you think had happened to Mahmoud?'

'When he left without even saying goodbye, I assumed he'd dumped me. I took it badly and dropped out of uni and went back home.'

'If you and Hossein were only passing acquaintances, how did he know where you were?' Aunt Jessica would have made a brilliant detective. No matter how good the story, if there were any inconsistencies, she'd spot them straight away.

'Through Pamela. She was the only person I kept in touch with after I left London. Strictly speaking, she kept in touch with me. She used to work as a waitress in the café where Mahmoud and I used to meet, and we became friends. She knew all the students and remained friends with a couple of the other Iranian boys who married English girls and stayed in London. Through them she learnt what Hossein was doing and she sent him my address. Not that I could tell him anything. I never heard anything from Mahmoud after he disappeared – either then or since.'

She took out her handkerchief and noisily blew her nose.

The suspense was driving me crazy.

'Then what happened?'

'It looked as though the family had drawn a blank trying to find Mahmoud, but Hossein decided to continue trying to track down Reza. He was convinced that he must know what happened, either because he was the SAVAK agent who betrayed him or because, as Mahmoud's cousin, he had helped smuggle him out of their clutches to America.

It took him some time and I've no doubt a fair amount of money changed hands, but Hossein discovered that Reza had made such a name for himself working for SAVAK while he was a student in London. He worked his way up the ranks of the organisation until he became quite senior. When the Pahlavi regime fell after the revolution, he was under threat from the resulting purge and had to escape the country overnight. He managed to get to Turkey, established himself with a new identity and nice little business running a high-class clothing factory in Ismir. He was so successful that over the years he bought and supplied a sizable chain of stores.'

Aunt Jessica frowned. 'But he'd need money to do that in the first place? Where did it come from?'

'That's exactly what Hossein wanted to know. The only suggestion he was given was that Reza might have been involved in smuggling heroin.' She shook her head. 'I was sceptical. I'd never liked Reza and he certainly didn't like me, but I just couldn't see him as a drug smuggler. Unlike the majority of the other students, he was a devout Muslim. He never drank alcohol or gambled and was always quick to give up those who did.'

My aunt and I exchanged looks, but this was not the time to ask if she knew the identity of the man in the photos. Instead, Aunt Jessica asked, 'If Reza is supposed to be in Turkey what was he doing on this tour with a British passport?'

'Hossein discovered that five years ago, he sold up his business, retired and left the area. That's when the information dried up, though there were hints that he might be back in England.'

The story was getting more complicated by the minute. My head was beginning to spin.

'Once I heard what Hossein had discovered, I decided to go back to Kensington and see if the café where we used to meet was still there.'

She started coughing. I collected the glass of water from

the front. It was part of the routine for me to fetch one for Aunt Jessica before her talk. Irene gladly gulped it down as we waited for the rest of the story.

'At first, I wasn't certain, people change a great deal in forty years, but after I'd been back a couple of times, I became certain that one of the regulars who used to sit at the same window table talking over old times was Reza.'

'He didn't recognise you?'

She snorted and shook her head. 'Back then, women were considered second class citizens as far as most Iranian men were concerned, especially British women. It was an open secret that he was a SAVAK agent, so we all kept a wary eye on him. Anyway, I was convinced it was him, and I became a regular customer. I'd take a book and sit at a nearby table listening in.'

'If you were so certain it was Reza, why didn't you tackle him? Ask him if he knew what had happened to Mahmoud?'

'What would have been the point? He would simply deny knowing what I was talking about.'

She licked her lips, picked up the glass of water again and took a large gulp.

'One day he turned up late. He was usually there by two o'clock – half past at the latest. I waited till three and was about to leave when Reza arrived in a bit of a state. He and his cronies went into a huddle. I could only catch the odd phrase, but Reza said something about not having a choice. His father was dying. One of his mates protested that it was too dangerous for him to go back to Iran, but Reza tapped his nose and said he had insurance. He gave that same nasty smile. That's when I was certain it had to be Reza. I remember that smirk from when he told me all those years ago that Mahmoud had left London and I would never see him again.' She gave an involuntary shudder.

'But what I still don't understand,' I persisted, 'is how you and he just happened to come to be together in Iran on the same holiday.'

'A lucky break really. A couple of days later, Reza told his friends he'd booked on a holiday tour to Iran in November.'

'If his life was in danger, it stands to reason he was less likely to be noticed among a group of British tourists than arriving as an individual passenger,' Aunt Jessica said.

Irene nodded. 'Hossein and I came to the same conclusion.'

'But how did you find out which tour he'd be on?'

'One of his mates asked when he was leaving. Once I had the exact date, it wasn't too difficult to track down the correct tour and which company he was using.'

'That was a lucky coincidence,' I muttered, but they both ignored me.

'So you decided to book on it as well?' Aunt Jessica persisted.

'No. At least not at first. When I told Hossein, he confirmed that a group leaving from Heathrow were due to arrive at his hotel on the same day. As the departure date grew closer, I became more and more keyed up. I couldn't just sit on the side-lines, so I made a late booking and joined the tour. Hossein wasn't expecting me, and he was none too pleased. Said I could blow the whole thing if Reza recognised me from the café. I didn't think there was much chance of that. Not with a scarf wrapped round my head.'

'I presume that you and Hossein intended to use the fact that Reza was in Iran posing as a Turkish tourist to blackmail him into telling you what he knew about Mahmoud's disappearance and where he might be now.'

'Exactly. But he died before we had the chance to speak to him.'

I looked at my watch and stood up. 'Much as I hate to break this up, ladies, but it's almost dinner time and I need to get all this stuff upstairs.'

Aunt Jessica turned back to me. 'If you can manage

everything else, I'll return the glass and meet you in the dining-room.'

The two women left me to finish packing up the laptop and projector and putting the leads in their bag.

CHAPTER 27

The previous evening's revelations had left me more confused than ever. Irene's story had been so convoluted that it made my head spin just trying to sort out the details. If neither she nor Mr Kamali were involved in the death of Yusef then who was responsible? The deed itself could not have been done by any of the other passengers on our tour because they were all walking in the street. On the other hand, why would whoever ordered Yusef's fatal accident want to injure Irene and kidnap Mr Kamali? How would he even know what the pair of them were up to? All this time, I'd been lining up suspects in our tour party but now I wasn't so sure.

I was still trying to make sense of things as I buttoned up my shirt when there was a knock at my door.

Aunt Jessica stood there a big smile on her face.

'I'm not late, am I?' I was usually the one who called for her before breakfast.

'No, sweetie. I just wanted to give you these before we go down. Happy birthday! The top one's from me and the others are from the rest of the family.' She kissed my cheek then thrust a handful of envelopes into my hands and pushed me inside. 'You'll have to wait for your presents till we get back home. My case was heavy enough without carting them all the way over here.'

I sat on my bed and opened my cards. Predictably, Aunt Jessica's was a comic one but those from my mother, Aunt Maud and Aunt Edwina were the traditional "pretty" type with flowers, butterflies or birds. I was quite touched that my cousin Patricia, Edwina's daughter, had also sent one. Two rather cute kittens looking not dissimilar from her own black and white pet, the love of her life.

'I'd forgotten all about my birthday.'

I stood, planted a kiss on her cheek and arranged the cards on the table below the wall-mounted television.

'I hope you haven't told the rest of the party. The last thing I want is to be made a fuss of.'

'That's why I gave you them to you here rather than embarrass you by presenting them at breakfast.'

Several of the others were already in the restaurant by the time we arrived.

'Here comes the birthday boy!' cried Barbara.

Everyone turned and looked at me, wishing me happy returns of the day. I glared at Aunt Jessica but before I could accuse her, she put up her hands and shook her head.

'Don't blame me. I haven't told anyone.'

Barbara giggled. 'Aahil told us.'

'So how did he find out?' I muttered to Aunt Jessica as we sat down at the large table.

'From your passport, I expect,' she said.

Much to my relief, I was not the centre of attention for too long. After the pictures they'd seen at last evening's lecture, everyone was excited at the prospect of visiting the magnificent World Heritage square Shah Abbas had built as a polo ground, his palace and the stunning Persian blue tiled mosques arranged around it.

'Isfahan certainly looks like a photographer's paradise. I just hope I have enough space left. I'm down to my last card,' said Gordon.

'That's the least of my problems,' moaned Barbara. 'If we're out all day, I'm not sure my camera battery will last. It died on me that day we went to Persepolis. I never thought to buy a spare before we came.'

'It might help if you resisted the temptation to keep checking the photos you've already taken,' suggested Robert.

I nodded in agreement.

As it turned out, we started the day not in the main Naqsh-e Jahan Square itself but just off it to see what Aahil described as a summer palace and garden.

'It never ceases to amaze me how you arrive at these high forbidding walls and firmly shut plain wooden gates only to go inside to see these extensive gardens and great long lakes leading up to a pavilion at the far end,' said Irene as we waited for the tailenders to join us. 'Standing here, with all those tall trees at the sides and extending into the distance you can't even see the walls. It's all so spacious, yet it's right in the heart of the city.'

It took some time to stroll down the path alongside the wide water channel admiring the occasional statuary before we reached the palace itself. I stopped to take more photos and Irene walked alone. I wasn't worried for her safety. Not here. We were the only party that had been allowed in. For some reason the place was closed for the day, but we had special permission. Whether he had arranged it with management, or it was done through the company, Aahil didn't say. Even though I was confident no harm could come to her here, I still couldn't shake off the feeling that not all the rest of the party were innocent. Yusef's death, Irene's accident and Hossein's disappearance were evidence that whatever lay behind all this involved more than one person. It stood to reason that they had to have at least one person on the inside and that could only be one of our party.

I'd been so lost in thought as I made my way to the long low pavilion ahead, still trying to make sense of Irene's latest revelations that it was only when I was much closer that I realised how much more impressive it was close up. Massive wooden columns held up the flat roof to provide a shaded terrace in front of the entrance. From a distance I'd seen only six, but I realised there were two more rows behind. They were what had given the palace its name – Chehel Cotun or Forty Columns. There were supposed to be twenty in all, though I could only count eighteen. The rest were the reflections in the water.

Delicate patterns in blue, orange and white tile decorated the frieze at the top of the terrace and ceiling was also tiled in a variety of geometric patterns. Spectacular though it was, it paled into insignificance once I followed the rest of the party through the arched entrance into the first hall. The twinkling glare from the mirror mosaics which covered every surface almost hurt the eyes. By the time I'd finished taking photographs, I'd been left behind.

Aahil was well into his spiel by the time I followed the party into the main reception hall. I made no attempt to catch them up.

The palace was built as a grand hall where the shah could receive and entertain foreign ambassadors and dignitaries. I wondered if those eminent visitors had stood stock still, staring open-mouthed like me trying to take it all in.

The ceiling rose in a series of arched domes along the length of the hall, each geometrical section intricately painted predominantly in orange, giving a warm amber glow to the whole vast space. The upper walls were covered in magnificent murals each one featuring hundreds of life-sized figures. The colours so bright, they could have been painted yesterday.

For once, I decided to feast my eyes first rather than take photos. That could come later.

I wasn't the only one left behind when the party moved on outside. Phil was a keen photographer as I knew well.

'I hope Helen made lots of notes. I missed all of Aahil's explanation,' he said.

'So did I. That's why I am also photographing all the information boards. Though by the looks of things, that could take me a good few hours to digest when I get back home.'

'There's a very Indian style to many of these paintings, don't you think?'

'I seem to remember my aunt saying something about the Safavids having a good relationship with India. It was the Ottomans they went to war with.'

'I suppose that explains the elephants in this picture.'

Together we continued down the second side of the room, chatting as we went and as we made our way outside, he said, 'Irene seems a bit subdued this morning. I saw the two of you talking earlier. Is she alright?'

'I think so. Just a bit tired that's all. It's hot out here and this holiday is pretty full on.'

'You have a point. We certainly pack in the days, on the go all the time. It is pretty exhausting. You seem to be keeping a protective eye on her. I wondered if you knew her from before you came out here?'

I shook my head. 'No. I was a bit concerned about her, that's all. That tumble down the stairs shook her up a lot more than she tries to make out.'

'You could be right.'

Aahil was leading the rest of the group around the back wall of the building, identifying the various figures on the painted wall. Phil went off to join his wife and I made my way to the little group gathered around Aunt Jessica a short distance away.

Was it my imagination or had Phil engineered our little chat so he could sound me out? Could he be the inside man or was I getting paranoid, reading all sorts in intrigue in perfectly innocent conversations?

CHAPTER 28

It was only a short walk from the Pavilion Gardens to the main historic square which was prohibited to traffic. Aahil suggested that before we visited the Aali Qapu Palace, we take a short coffee break.

'The café I'm taking you to is the best spot from which to take a photo of the whole square.'

He led us right down to the north end next to the entrance of the bazaar. There were a few groans from the older ladies when they realised that they had to climb several flights of steep steps to reach the terrace, but the result was definitely worth the effort.

From this high vantage point, the whole length of the square with its patchwork of lawns, paths and water features flanked by an arcade of shops lay before us right down to the Abbasi Great Mosque at the far end.

'Is that the Royal Palace? About halfway down on the right,' asked Mary pointing to a squarish building with an enormous, canopied balcony that dominated the skyline.

'It must be,' I answered. 'Didn't Aahil mention something about it being opposite Shah Abbas's private mosque? If you look over on the left, you can see its great blue dome.'

'Oh yes.' She turned to her husband. 'Do you see all those little pony and traps taking people round the square? They look fun.'

Gordon gave her an indulgent smile. 'I know Aahil said we had some free time at the end, but if you want to look round all those shops, you might have to choose. But right now, he's about to start his talk so if you want to hear what he has to say we'd better go and join the others.'

'This square is one of the largest in the world,' said Aahil. 'When Shah Abbas decided to make Isfahan the capital of his empire, it was built not just to demonstrate the wealth and magnificence of his rule but to bring together politics, religion and business. From his palace he could keep an eye on everything that was happening. As Jessica told you in her lecture, he needed to keep on the right side of the clerics. Their support was essential to legitimise his rule. Not only did he marry his daughter to a cleric, he ordered the building of the magnificent mosque you see at the far end. It was the crown jewel of Safavid architecture as I'll show you later.

'The wealth of the empire depended on trade, so he built the city on the great Silk Route and established the Imperial Bazaar, the largest market of its time. During the day, much of the square itself would be occupied by the tents of the merchants and the tradesmen. In the evening there would be entertainers, and people would come to eat and drink.'

'But didn't Jessica tell us the Shah had polo matches and great parades in the square?'

'Indeed, he did. The square was cleared for public ceremonies and national festivities such as at New Year. Polo not only originated here in Persia, it was the national sport and was enjoyed not only by the Shah and his guests but by the ordinary people.'

As everyone went to sit down, only the most enthusiastic photographers were left at the edge of the terrace. As this was Aunt Jessica's fourth visit to Iran as accompanying historian, she already had a large library of photos from her previous trips, so she was the first to find a couple of seats and order coffees for us both. Probably just as well because she'd already drunk half her cappuccino by the time I'd finished clicking away.

'Thanks for this,' I said as I laid the camera carefully on the ledge alongside our small table before unclipping the waist strap of my heavy lenses case and lifting the shoulder strap over my head. It was too large to sit on the ledge, so I put it on the floor by my chair.

After a few comments about the fantastic views, I dropped my voice and said, 'It's busy in the square. It's going to be impossible to keep an eye on Irene especially when we all go our separate ways later on.'

Aunt Jessica looked across the terrace to one of the tables on the far side. 'I don't think you need worry about that too much. She and Barbara have teamed up again and I've no doubt they'll wander off together when the time comes. Let's wait and see.'

'You could be right.' I took a sip of my rapidly cooling coffee. 'That reminds me, earlier when nearly everyone left the Pavilion and I was still taking photos, Phil was asking about Irene. He wanted to know if I knew her from before the trip.'

'Oh. What gave him that idea?'

'He said it was because I seemed to have taken her under my wing, though why he singled me out, I can't imagine.'

'No, it does seem a bit odd. I'd have thought Barbara would have been a more obvious choice for that particular role. The two of them have been almost inseparable especially since her fall.'

'So, what's he up to? Was he warning me off, do you think?'

'Off what?'

'Assuming that pushing Irene down the stairs was a warning for her not to interfere, could it be a veiled attempt to tell me to keep my distance.'

'That's a bit of a leap, even for you. First Robert now Phil. You're beginning to see conspiracies everywhere. The man was most likely simply making conversation.'

'If only we knew why Irene and Hossein Kamali have been targeted, we might begin to solve this riddle. It can't be to stop them talking to Yusef or Reza whatever his name was. He was dead before any of this happened. Is there something Irene still isn't telling us? Her story is a bit…' I struggled to find the right word, 'confusing. Farfetched, even. As though she was making it up as she went along.'

'Complicated, I'll grant you, but I think she's telling the truth. Just not the whole story. However, I doubt we'll ever find the solution to all this until we've answered a far more basic question. Assuming Yusef was over here because of his dying father, even though he was well aware of the danger he faced by returning to Iran, what was the insurance that he brought with him?'

'Could it have something to do with those photos we found?'

'More than likely, I'd say.'

'What's the next step? Ask Irene if she recognises the guy at the nightclub?'

She ran her tongue along her bottom lip, making up her mind. 'I'm not sure. Showing the picture around could be dangerous.'

If Aunt Jessica had any alternative ideas, there was no time for her to share them with me because Aahil was rounding us up to take us to the palace. I paid little attention to the goods displayed in shop windows that drew oohs and aahs from those around me as we made our way. Not that I came up with any answers either.

By the time we reached the balcony on the third floor of the compact high-rise Aali Qapu Palace, I'd given up trying, and after taking a few more photos, went to hear the rest of what Aahil was saying.

'…underground tunnel for the Shah to reach his own private mosque on the far side of the square.'

The stairs to the upper floors were, like the rest of the building, ridiculously steep. Barbara, Irene, Mary and Gordon decided they had had enough and stayed on the balcony.

'Is it really worth the climb?' Helen asked Aunt Jessica.

'Oh yes. The finest reception rooms where the Shah entertained all the visiting ambassadors is right at the top. It's known as the music room.'

Helen didn't look convinced. 'Maybe, but you have long legs. It's not so easy for us who aren't so lucky.'

'The stucco work is well worth seeing.'

'Righty-ho. On your head be it. I'll expect you to pull me up that last flight if needs be.'

Laughing together the two women turned to the stairs with the rest of us following on.

After our visit to the Shah's elaborately decorated private mosque where every inch of the building's interior walls and ceilings were covered in tilework and even the marble floors were intricately patterned, the stark plain walls of the inner corridors in the Great Mosque came as a surprise. Stout brick pillars rose to support the arches holding up the ceilings. They possessed all the awe and grandeur of English Norman cathedrals drawing the eye up to the brickwork patterns in the ribbed domed roofs.

Nor had I appreciated that the complex would be quite so large. The vast size of the place meant that I dare not take too long trying to get the perfect shot in case I became separated from the rest of the party. There were crowds of gawping tourists winding their way through the corridors surrounding a large open central courtyard. In the courtyard, there were four great portals, one on each side. Even in the main prayer hall, only the section surrounding the mihrab niche was tiled.

When we eventually found ourselves outside again in a garden at the back of the complex, Aahil said he had a special treat in store for us.

'We are now in the religious school built by Shah Abbas when he made the city his capital. Around the garden you see the rooms for the students. Today, you are lucky. Few tourists are privileged to be able to speak to the manager of the school. If you wait here a moment, I will inform him you are here.'

A tall, slim, strikingly handsome man in clerical robes appeared with Aahil almost at once. He was probably in his early forties and exuded a quiet authority which had us all hanging on his every word. His English was fluent and with no trace of an accent. He talked about the school's history, its courses and students, not all of whom went on to become clerics. At the end, he was happy to answer questions.

They came thick and fast until Aahil interrupted. 'We must not keep the manager away from his work. Perhaps one last question.'

Before anyone else jumped in, Caroline asked, 'Is it only men who come to the school?'

'No. We do have girls, but they are taught separately and by women in another area of the school.'

The poor man looked decidedly uncomfortable and hurried away before anyone had a chance to ask any more questions he did not want to answer.

CHAPTER 29

'That was fascinating,' I said as we all trooped after Aahil back into the main square.

Aunt Jessica gave me one of her looks. 'The manager certainly caught your eye.'

I raised an eyebrow. 'You have to admit, he was enough to stir every woman's passion. Even his voice had a magnetic quality.'

She gave me a cheeky grin. 'With that I would have to agree.'

'I wonder what it is that makes the men and women in this part of the world so attractive.'

'Being so lithe and slim helps but I think it's the way they carry themselves. There's a regal quality to the way they move that draws attention.'

Aahil gathered us all together to point out the low stone pillar – all that remained of the original polo ground – where we were all to meet up again later.

'I'm afraid our last visit went on for a little longer than I'd planned but the coach will be waiting for us so I'd still like you all to be back here at five o'clock.'

As everyone headed off, I looked around to find Irene who I spotted going into the arcade. With my arm tucked in Aunt Jessica's, I quickened my pace to follow her.

'Slow down.'

'I want…'

'To keep an eye on Irene. Yes. I realise that, but she

won't thank you if she realises what you're up to. Besides, she'll be fine. Barbara's with her.'

'But...'

'We can keep our distance. Just follow at a more leisurely pace. Besides, I still want to buy some boxes of sweets to take back. We're off home in a few more days and there's not much more opportunity to shop.'

'Or to solve our mystery.'

'True.'

After a quarter of an hour or so, we caught up with Irene and Barbara looking in a shop window crammed full of blue enamelware.

'I know they're pricey, but those intricate patterns are so lovely I've decided I'm going to treat myself to a small piece, but I can't make up my mind between that little pot with diamond shapes in Persian blue and turquoise or that one at the bottom with flowery patterns in lozenges. Irene's no help. What do you two think?'

'Whoa,' I said taking a step back hands in the air. 'Don't ask me. I'm a mere man. No taste when it comes to such things. I'm going into the sweet shop next door. I need to get some goodies to take back as pressies.'

'What a good idea!' said Irene. 'I'll come with you. Why don't you go back inside, Barbara? Take Jessica with you. Have another look round and then when you've made your decision you can come and join us.'

Getting Irene on her own was a bonus I hadn't expected. I have to admit, Aunt Jessica is always much more adept at wheedling information out of people than I'll ever be, but, with time so short, this was not an opportunity I could afford to miss. For a couple of minutes, I busied myself looking at the attractively boxed sweet selection while I tried to think of how I could bring up the topic.

Irene suddenly let out a sob. She quickly tried to disguise it as a cough. I put a hand on her shoulder.

'You still haven't heard from Hossein, I take it?'

She shook her head.

'It's hard keeping up a pretence all the time. Barbara is very kind and I'm sure she suspects something is wrong, but she probably thinks I'm still getting over my fall.'

'You haven't been tempted to tell her?'

'Oh no. Only you and Jessica have any idea of what's been going on. Not that I can make any sense of it myself. Do you think the people who've taken Hossein are the same ones who killed Yusef?'

'We don't know Hossein has been taken at all. He could just be hiding, or it might be something else entirely. There's no reason to think the worst.' I tried to sound as positive as possible, and she did manage a weak smile.

She patted my arm. 'You're a kind boy.'

Now was as good an opportunity as I was going to get. 'Actually, Irene, there's something I've been wondering about. I know you said that you didn't actually see the accident, but you were right behind Yusef just before he stepped off the pavement. Did you by any chance hear who was calling him? Did he mention a name?'

Irene frowned and shook her head. 'I wasn't paying much attention.'

'Strange though to get a phone call at that time of day when you're supposed to be on holiday. He was on his mobile when he first arrived. I noticed him on the coach going to the hotel. Do you think it could be the same person calling him?'

She shrugged. 'Possibly.'

'Can you remember how he reacted? Did he sound as if he was expecting the call, or was he surprised?'

'I've no idea.'

'What language was he speaking?'

Irene took her time answering. 'I can't swear to it, but I don't think it was English. Farsi or Turkish perhaps. I wouldn't know the difference. Do you think it's important?'

'Probably not. Did you notice what happened to the phone after the accident? Did he drop it or was he still holding it?'

'No idea. But I do know he never had time to put it in his pocket because he was still talking when the car hit him.'

At that moment Barbara came bustling into the shop eager to show us all the little lidded pot she'd chosen. Any chance of probing any further was at an end.

Back at the hotel, it took me some time to download all the photos I'd taken that day. I was still at it when Aunt Jessica knocked on my door.

'I've just counted up,' I told her. 'I thought I'd taken a record number the day we went to Persepolis, but do you realise there's nearly three hundred and fifty pictures here!'

She chuckled as she plonked herself down on my bed. 'That should keep you busy when we get back home.'

'It'll take several days just to look through them all properly let alone sort out the ones I'd like to enhance.'

'I don't like to rush you, sweetie, but we're all supposed to be meeting Aahil down in the lobby in just over half an hour. Isn't it time you started thinking about getting yourself ready?'

'Is he taking us out for dinner tonight?'

'No. He said everyone is probably too tired after today. We were on our feet the whole time. Seems they do good bar meals in the main lounge on the ground floor, so he suggested we eat there. We're going out somewhere special tomorrow night as it's effectively our last. Saturday, we'll be travelling back to Tehran.'

'Okay-dokey. Give me five minutes and I'll be with you.'

The lounge was just off to the right of the hotel entrance. The twelve of us sat together at the side of the room. The bar menu was relatively limited and not particularly interesting and, in the end, I settled for a venison burger and chips.

I'd more or less finished eating when I noticed a local

woman peering in through the open doorway. Her Persian blue skirts brushed the floor, and her plain pale blue scarf almost hid her dark hair. Her eyes kept darting around the room as though she was looking for someone. Eventually, her gaze settled on our group. I didn't want her to catch me staring at her, so I looked away.

'I don't suppose they do puddings in here, do they?' I asked.

Caroline, who was sitting opposite me on the bench seat that ran under the high curtained windows, gave a knowing look and said, 'I don't think you'll need any dessert. There's something coming.'

Before I could ask what she meant, everyone started clapping as they looked towards the bar. I looked over my shoulder to see Hassan approaching bearing aloft an enormous cake. It had to be eighteen inches square. In the centre was a single candle, but it was shooting tiny stars like an oversized sparkler on Guy Fawkes night.

There were cries of happy birthday and Caroline and Aunt Jessica began clearing a space on the low table. With great ceremony, Hassan laid it in front of me. It was covered in chocolate buttercream with swirls piped around the edge sprinkled with chocolate flakes.

'Come on, Harry! Blow it out.'

I wasn't even sure that it was possible but, feeling very foolish, I took a deep breath, leant forward lips pursed. It might only have been just the one candle, but it took every ounce of puff to accomplish it and even then, I'm not certain if it didn't fizzle out of its own accord. By that time everyone was singing Happy Birthday at the tops of their voices. I was grateful I had my back to the rest of the lounge bar occupants as the commotion the group were making must have turned every head in the room to see what was going on.

Once the singing died down, Aahil was at my shoulder with a large envelope and a box in a pretty red and purple paisley-patterned paper bag.

'This is from everyone.'

It wasn't a conventional birthday card. It had a picture of a mosque taken at night and inside, everyone had signed it, most with short little messages. The bag contained a tin of sweetmeats.

'A big, big thank you, everyone.'

I could feel my cheeks burning at all the attention and muttered at Aunt Jessica who was sitting next to me, 'I'll get you for this.'

She laughed. 'Nothing to do with me. I knew nothing about it. You'll see Aahil didn't even ask me to sign the card.'

'What am I supposed to do with this? Is there a knife around to cut it with?'

'I think Hassan is waiting to return it to the chef who will cut it up for you,' Aahil explained.

Two minutes later Hassan and Ali appeared carrying trays of small plates and a pile of paper napkins and began handing them out.

'These slices are enormous!' cried Helen. 'I'll never eat all this.'

To say the cake was rich is something of an understatement. The four layers of sponge were separated by thick layers of butter cream, never mind the topping. Even with my sweet tooth, I was pushed to finish it.

Looking at the row of plates lying on the tables, some with only barely half-eaten portions, I said, 'I was planning to open my tin of sweets and pass them round when we'd finished dinner, but I somehow doubt I'll get many takers.'

'I need a coffee after that,' said Aunt Jessica as she delicately licked the last of the icing from her fingertips.

'Me too.'

I glanced around and waved at one of the waiters.

Our coffees weren't the only thing to arrive. Hassan appeared with a tray of more slices of birthday cake.

'You give everyone second slice.'

'I very much doubt it they'll want one. Why don't you and Ali and the waiting staff have it?'

He gave me one of his beaming smiles. 'We already have!'

He thrust the tray into my hands and was gone before I had a chance to send it back.

The only person I could persuade to take a slice was Robert. 'I'll take another piece to eat later.'

The lounge was beginning to fill up, so I managed to persuade a few guests at the nearby tables to take one, but I still had plenty left. I caught the eye of the woman in the blue dress standing in the doorway.

'Would you like a slice?'

She was much older than I'd first thought, her dark hair peppered with grey. She ignored the tray I was holding out and said, 'You with group come from England?'

'That's right. We landed in Tehran nearly a fortnight ago.'

'You come with Yusef?'

It certainly wasn't the question I was expecting and when I didn't answer straight away, she asked again. 'Yusef in your party, yes? Why he not here? He not phone me.'

Realisation dawned. 'You must be his sister. I'm sorry to tell you, he was involved in a traffic accident.'

Her hands flew to her face and her eyes widened when I explained. After the initial shock, what I read in them was not so much sorrow for a dead brother but fear. Abject fear.

'But he bring me… He promise.'

I thought for a moment she was about to collapse but as I went to put out a steadying arm, she pulled back.

'Where his things?'

'They have all been sent back to England.'

She looked over my left shoulder and her body went rigid. I turned to see what had provoked such a dramatic reaction. There was nothing unusual that I could see. I turned back to ask her what the problem was, but she was already at the entrance. The woman was clearly agitated about more than her brother's death. I hurried to the doors but there was no sign of her. She had disappeared into the night.

CHAPTER 30

All eyes turned on me when I returned.

'Was that woman bothering you?' asked Robert.

'Not at all. I offered her a piece of cake,' I said as I laid the plate back on the table and went to sit down.

'You were talking for a long time.'

His insistence made me wary. 'Not really. She seemed very shy. Didn't have much English so I wasn't sure if she understood me or was refusing out of politeness. I was trying to explain it was my birthday, telling her it was an English custom to offer cake to people.'

'Given the way she took off like that, you can't have made too good a job of it.'

Even Caroline looked askance at her husband's snide comment.

Before I could think of a suitable reply my mobile started ringing. It was a good opportunity to escape on the pretext that it was getting noisy in the lounge.

Even when I moved out into the lobby, a steady flow of people kept coming into the lounge. It was just gone nine o'clock. The restaurant was probably closing and the last of the diners had come down to the bar to socialise for the rest of the evening.

I retreated outside the hotel doors where it was a good deal quieter.

'Happy birthday, darling.'

'Thanks, Mum. Sorry I took so long to answer. I was in the lounge and it was a bit noisy in there, so I've come outside. The tour guide arranged a wonderful surprise birthday cake for me.'

'I haven't called at a bad moment, have I? I didn't mean to drag you away from all your friends, especially if you're having a party.'

'No, it's fine, Mum. Honestly. You should have seen the cake though. It was huge. Would feed an army.'

'Did you take a picture?'

'I was too surprised. I wasn't expecting it, but other people took one of me trying to blow out the candle. I'll get someone to give me a copy and then I'll be able to show you.'

The conversation went on for another five or ten minutes and I went back to re-join the others.

'I assume that was your mother,' said Aunt Jessica. 'Did you ask how Maud was faring?'

'I spoke to her. She sounds like her old self. Actually, a good deal nicer to me than she usually is but then, it is my birthday, so I expect she was making a special effort.'

This was not the place for me to tell Aunt Jessica about Yusef's sister, much as I was dying to do so. It would not look good for the two of us to disappear now. Not after Aahil had arranged the evening in my honour, so to speak.

It must have been roughly half an hour later that we became aware of a rumpus going on just outside the hotel.

'Was that a police siren or an ambulance?'

Barbara who had no qualms about appearing nosey was kneeling up on the bench seat, head under the thick plush curtains peering out of the window and intent on giving us a running commentary.

'An ambulance and a couple of police cars with lights flashing have just driven past but I think they must have stopped close by because I can still see the glow from their lights and the noise they're making is as loud as ever.'

'Accident most like,' came Phil's deep boom from the far end of the table.

'Iran does seem to have crazy drivers,' said Helen.

Aunt Jessica and I exchanged glances. I wondered if she was experiencing the same sense of foreboding that was chilling my spine.

Barbara was the first to spot them in the lobby.

'The police are in the hotel. It has to be something to do with what's going on outside.' She leant forward and continued in a loud whisper, 'Do you think it's one of the guests who's been knocked down?'

It was impossible to tell what was going on from where we were sitting. I presumed the police were talking to the management and the receptionists.

I glanced at my watch. 'It's ten o'clock and I'd rather like to get to bed, but it would look as if I was being nosey if I went out there now.'

'Let's give it another ten minutes,' said Aunt Jessica.

The two of us were already on our feet when three uniformed officers appeared in the doorway accompanied by the hotel doorman. The doorman discreetly nodded in the direction of our table then scuttled off back to his duties.

One of the officers, presumably the senior man, walked over to our table.

'Forgive me for disturbing your evening, ladies and gentlemen. You are all English, I understand?'

We all nodded like guilty school children, uncertain what we were about to be accused of.

'Can you tell me if any of you noticed a local woman dressed in blue in the hotel earlier this evening?'

'She was standing in the doorway,' piped up Barbara.

'Did any of the rest of you notice her?' Most of the group raised a hand.

'Did anyone speak to her?'

'I did. Just briefly. There was some cake left over,' I pointed to the tray still lying on the table, 'and I was offering it around to everyone rather than have it wasted.'

His eyes narrowed. I had the distinct feeling I was about to be accused of something.

A sudden burst of laughter from a noisy group of Italian tourists over by the bar drowned his next question.

'I'm sorry, officer. I didn't quite catch that.'

He gave a snort then said, 'It might be best if we find somewhere a little quieter to continue our conversation.'

I felt like saying it appeared more like an interrogation than a conversation, but rather than protest and make the situation any worse, I followed him out to the lobby. One of the other officers fell into step behind me. I was marched through the lobby and shown into a small empty office alongside the reception desk. As none of the hotel staff challenged him and all the receptionists busied themselves as I walked past, I presumed the temporary 'interview' room had been set aside earlier.

Once all three of us were seated, the senior man said, 'I am Inspector Ahmadi. And you are?'

'Harry Hamilton-James.'

Out of the corner of my eye, I notice the other officer writing it down.

'You approached her. Not the other way around?'

I nodded. 'As I said, I was handing out cake.'

'But why go all the way to the lobby and not to the nearer tables?'

'I'd already asked everyone at the tables closest to us and I still had some left. I happened to catch her eye and I thought she might like a piece.'

'Did she accept your offer?'

'Well no, actually.'

'So what happened next?'

'She asked if I was English. We've met several local people who like to speak to British and American visitors to practice their English. We exchanged a couple of sentences, then she left the hotel.'

'Did you go after her?'

'No. Why would I? I went back to the rest of my party.'

'But you were seen leaving the hotel.'

'No. When I sat down my phone rang. It was noisy in the lounge as you've just seen. I went into the lobby to take my call and then went outside. I'll admit I walked down the steps and sat on the low garden wall outside the hotel window. I was in sight of the hotel doors the whole time.'

'Can anyone verify that?'

'I've no idea. Why would they need to?' I had a strong inclination to lick my lips, but I was determined to stare him out and give no indication of the nervousness I felt inside.

'Because the body of the lady in question has been discovered a few hundred yards from here and you are the last person seen talking to her.'

CHAPTER 31

Aunt Jessica was the first person I saw when I was eventually released by the two police officers. She stood up and walked towards me, falling into step beside me as we continued to the lift.

Neither of us spoke. Her just being there with me was all the support I needed at that moment. Questions could wait until we were in the privacy of my room. My hand was still shaking as I extracted my key card from my jacket pocket and waved it vainly over the sensor. Gently she took it from me, turned it over and pushed open the door.

It took a couple of minutes before the tension began to subside.

'Want to talk about it?'

'I really thought I was going to be arrested.'

She smiled and patted my knee. 'But you weren't.'

'No, but the last thing he said was that he might want to talk to me again later. He made it very clear I'm not off the hook.'

After that everything came out in a confused jumble, but she didn't interrupt. Only when I'd finished did she ask, 'Did the woman tell you she was Yusef's sister?'

'No, but she didn't deny it when I said it.'

'Did you tell the Inspector who she was?'

I thought about it for a moment. 'I didn't really get much chance. Should I have done do you think?'

It was a moment or two before she shook her head.

'Even if that was why she was killed, I doubt the police

would have believed you. As far as they're concerned it's pure speculation on your part. There's no proof.'

'But after what happened to Yusef and Irene…'

'Both of which everyone else considers accidents.'

'But there has to be a connection.' Even I was aware of the high-pitched whine in my voice.

'I agree. Did this woman tell you what she wanted? Why she came to the hotel?'

'She obviously had no idea he was dead. I had the impression he was going to give her something. She asked what had happened to his things and when I told her they'd all been sent back to England, she looked devastated. I could be wrong, but she seemed more upset about that than her brother being killed. Do you think it's tied up to the photos on that USB stick?'

'That seems the most likely. Did you tell her you had it?'

'I didn't get the chance. Something spooked her. Something she spotted behind me. Then she just bolted out of the hotel before I had a chance to ask.'

'Something or someone?'

'I've no idea.'

'The trouble with this whole business is that as soon as you discover the answer to one question, two more pop up. If we assume the reason Reza risked coming back to Iran was to give a set of photos to his sister, why couldn't he just send it by post or email in the first place? Why did he need to deliver them in person?'

'I suppose both are easy to intercept.'

'There has to be more to it than that.' She shook her head. 'There's also the question of what was she going to do with them.'

'I know we talked about blackmail when I first found the pictures, but she didn't give me the impression she was out to make money out of them. More like she needed them for protection. Could she have been threatened – *you get those photos from your brother or else!*'

She looked at me askance, but she didn't dismiss my

idea.

'One thing is certain. It's more important than ever that we discover the identity of the man in the photos.'

'So where do we start? After what's just happened, it could be dangerous to start flashing that picture around. We've no idea whom we can trust.'

'Exactly. Which is why we need to start on the internet. There's no certainty that Reza actually took the photos, but I'm prepared to bet my mother's pearls that they were taken while he was at university in London in the late '70s. Where's your laptop?'

I grabbed it from beneath a pile of shirts in the second drawer and fired it up. It took an age to warm up after I'd entered the hotel internet login and password.

'Now what?'

'Type in "Grosvenor Soho in 1970s" and click on images.'

There was nothing of any help there nor in any of the next dozen combinations of words we tried. It was long gone mid-night when we decided to call it a day.

I leant back trying to ease the crick in the back of my neck and shoulders after being huddled over the laptop cradled on my knees for so long.

Even Aunt Jessica who'd been sat beside me staring at the screen, gave a full body stretch when she stood up.

'After a traumatic end to what was already a busy day, you need a good night's rest. Let's hope one or other of us wakes up with some inspiration.'

She bent down, kissed the top of my head and headed for the door. At the last minute, she turned.

'By the way, do we know who found the body?'

'The Inspector didn't say. Why? Is it relevant?'

'Probably not.'

CHAPTER 32

After a decent night's sleep, I woke feeling surprisingly chipper. I was dressed and ready a good five minutes before the time I'd arranged to call for Aunt Jessica. Rather than sit around and risk my worries creeping back to ruin my good mood, I decided to knock on her door.

'Morning. I'm a bit early…'

'Not a problem. Just let me fetch my scarf.'

I followed her in. 'Looks as though it's going to be another glorious day.'

'I'm not trying to burst your bubble, but you do realise you're about to face a barrage of questions when we go for breakfast. Have you thought about what you're going to tell them?'

'Not really. As little as possible, I suppose.'

Paula was the first to bring up the subject. 'Anyone heard any more about what happened last night? There's a rumour going round that someone was murdered.'

Seizing the opportunity, I waded in. The best way for me to dispel their curiosity was to give them my side of the story before anyone began implying I had to be a suspect. 'I don't know about murder, but the policeman who spoke to me said that a local woman had been found collapsed in the street just round the corner from the hotel. Some of you may have noticed her while we were having dinner. She was standing in the doorway. The reason the police wanted to speak to me was because I actually spoke to her.

I offered her some birthday cake.'

'When you didn't come back, we thought you must have been arrested.'

It was the mocking gleam in his eye when Robert said it that wound me up. I could've cheerfully knocked out those too-perfect teeth of his. Everyone assumed he'd been making a joke and I had little choice but to add my own chuckle to the general titters. 'Hardly! Why on earth would they think I was responsible?'

Five minutes later, as I stood at the breakfast buffet spooning some jam-like concoction onto the side of my plate, a thought suddenly struck me. I wasn't the only one who'd left the table last night. When I stood up to take my call from my mother, Robert's chair was empty. I hadn't noticed him going, or for that matter, exactly when he returned.

I wasted no time telling Aunt Jessica when we left the breakfast-room.

'I vaguely remember hearing him telling Caroline he needed a pee, but I've no idea how long he was gone. Did you notice?'

She shook her head.

'It wouldn't take long for someone to follow her out, stab her in the back and return to the hotel.'

'Then whoever did it would have been covered in blood, which rather lets him off the hook.'

'I wasn't either, but the police suspected me. And we don't know how she was killed. She might just as easily have been strangled.'

'Just because Robert went to the loo doesn't make him guilty. So did several other people, including Paula and Phil.'

'Maybe. But Robert seemed pretty keen to know what she and I had been talking about.'

'There's nothing to say the poor woman was killed by anyone of our party in any case. Even if her death is linked to Yusef's, which I'll grant you is ninety-nine percent likely, we know categorically that no one on our tour could have been driving the car that ran down her brother. They were all on the street.'

There was no more time to discuss things. We'd reached our floor. Aunt Jessica fished in her pocket for her key card and disappeared inside her room.

As I climbed on board the coach for another full day's tour of Isfahan, I made a firm resolution. Tomorrow we would spend the day travelling back to Tehran which meant that this was effectively the last day of our holiday. I was determined to make the most of what was left of my holiday and not spend it agonising about Yusef, his sister, Irene or Mr Kamali. No matter how many times I kept going over and over the mystery in my mind, I wasn't going to solve it so there was no point.

Isfahan turned out to be quite a cosmopolitan city with its own Armenian quarter dating back to the seventeenth century when Shah Abbas decided to move them to the city. He allowed them to build the Cathedral of Vank and the Bethlehem Church. It was in this section of the city that our day began.

'I'm not sure I've ever been in an Armenian cathedral before,' Barbara confided as we walked towards it. 'I presume it's Eastern Orthodox, but somehow it reminds me a bit of the Friday Mosque we saw yesterday, with the plain walls and that great turnip dome. It even has blue tilework around the entry archways.'

To my way of thinking the inside was even more influenced by Islamist architecture. The whole structure resembled an Islamic house of worship even down to an internal courtyard. Were it not for the four rondels of angels, the intricate decoration in the vast dome would not have looked out of place in a mosque. Only the enormous Byzantine-style biblical frescos that dominated every wall revealed any western influence and it was no surprise when

Aahil told us that the murals were the work of a Dutch painter.

The cathedral was dedicated to Joseph of Arimathea. Brought up in a traditional Church of England environment which for me included Sunday school, I was well up on all the legends of the man who gave his tomb to Christ and his journey to Glastonbury.

Despite my earlier determination to play tourist for the day, I hadn't reckoned on Paula scuppering my plans.

The city was famous for its beautiful bridges and our itinerary included Khajou Bridge or, as Aahil described it, the bridge of twenty-three arches. The coach dropped us off some way off so that we could walk along the river and appreciate the full span of its two-tier structure. As so frequently happened on this trip, I was so busy taking photos that I only caught snatches of Aahil's spiel though I did hear something about women washing carpets at the sluice gates that ran under the bridge.

Paula and I were the last to reach the bridge.

'Looks as though everyone's making their way across already. I can see my aunt walking with Irene.'

'True. The oldies seem to have taken the low route. How's about you and me going up to the next tier. We'll get much better photos from higher up.'

'Okey-dokey. Where are the stairs?'

'Just behind you. Race you to the top.' She was off before I had a chance to turn round.

I should have realised she had an ulterior motive to get me on my own. We were halfway across, standing in the octagonal pavilion before she started quizzing me. She might have been a bit more subtle in her approach than the police, but it felt like an interrogation, nonetheless. It started innocently enough.

'Did you hear Aahil talking about how the Shah used to watch polo matches on the river from this balcony?'

'Water polo?'

'No silly. The players stood in their boats with their

sticks.'

'Still can't see how that would work. All that splashing would overturn the boats.'

'You have a point. Does seem a bit odd. Perhaps I misheard him. Talking about odd; wasn't that a strange business that happened last night at the hotel' When I gave no response, she went on. 'Did the police tell you how she died?'

'The police never tell you anything.'

'Another accident, do you think?'

I shrugged.

'It really makes you think. All these dreadful accidents. First Yusef in Tehran on the first day of the holiday, then Irene falling downstairs. She was so lucky not to break a leg. Or her neck, come to that. And now to top it all, another fatality just outside our hotel. Makes you wonder if they're all connected in some way.'

'I don't see how,' I said quickly. Perhaps too quickly. 'Besides, the woman who died yesterday had nothing to do with our tour.'

'But she was in the hotel just before she died. And she was there in the lobby all the time we were eating. I spotted her trying to hide behind the plants. She never took her eyes from our group. I had the distinct impression she was desperate to speak to one of us.'

I put up my hands in protest. 'I admit I spoke to her, but I'd never met the woman before, and I had no idea who she was. I still don't…'

'Calm down. I never said you did! All I'm saying is, that from the way she was acting, I think she was expecting to meet someone.'

'All I can tell you is what I told the police last night. I offered her cake which she refused, and she asked me if I was English.'

CHAPTER 33

I had no chance to tell Aunt Jessica of my encounter with Paula until much later. We'd stopped at another ancient stone bridge across the river. Once again, I paid little attention to Aahil's account of its history but this time it had nothing to do with taking photos. It may well have been the oldest in the city, but a stone bridge is a bridge. I just wanted to start walking across so I could have a private word with Aunt Jessica.

The feeling must have been mutual because once we all started walking, she slipped her arm through mine, slowing us down until the others were out of earshot.

'Guess what,' she said before I had a chance to open my mouth. 'Hossein Kamali has been found.'

'Really!' I stopped in my tracks.

'Keep your voice down and keep walking,' she commanded. 'You'll attract attention.'

'Is he okay? What happened?'

'Irene had a phone call from his hotel this morning. It seems he was found badly beaten up in a backstreet alley in the early hours of yesterday morning.'

'Has Irene spoken to him?'

'No, no. Just before we left the hotel this morning, she had a phone call from his hotel. All they know so far is that he wasn't identified until late last night when he gained consciousness. Obviously, the hotel is still trying to get more news from the hospital, but it seems the police are still waiting to question him about exactly what happened.'

'Perhaps we'll get some answers now.'

'Let's hope so.'

'Changing the subject, did you get a chance to show Irene the photo from Yusef's stick?'

She screwed up her face. 'To be honest after she'd told me about Mr Kamali, it went straight out of my head.'

We'd reached the far side of the bridge. Tonight's farewell dinner promised to be a multi-course feast so by mutual consent, everyone decided to skip lunch. We'd been given half an hour for a loo break, and should anyone feel peckish, a chance to buy a sandwich. It wasn't the most salubrious of areas. Run down in fact. The paths were cracked and uneven and strewn with litter. We passed a few shops selling ice-cream, with sandwiches and cakes in glass-fronted stands but nothing that would induce me to cross the street to examine their wares even if they were all wrapped or packaged. Not after I'd seen one stallholder, batting away the flies from his produce with a grubby tea towel. Needless to say, when we reached the toilets the queue for the ladies was three times longer than for the men.

'Don't bother to wait for me. I'll see you back at the coach.'

When I reached the bridge, I could see that Hassan had moved the coach which was now parked at the foot of the steps leading down from the bridge. Ahead of me I spotted Aahil and quickened my pace to catch him up. I fingered the phone in my pocket. I had half a mind to show him the head and shoulders shot from Yusef's USB stick I'd transferred from the laptop onto my mobile. Aunt Jessica wouldn't approve but time was getting short. Despite my earlier resolution to admit defeat and concentrate on my holiday, the thought of having to return home without ever solving this mystery was driving me crazy. Reluctantly, I took my hand out of my pocket. If there was a Mr Big out there, who better to be an inside man than Aahil?

'Hi there.'

Aahil looked over his shoulder and waited for me to catch up.

'Just wanted to ask what's next on the agenda.'

He laughed and pointed to Hassan and Ali standing behind the small table set up at the end of the bridge. 'Coffee time.'

'Hassan looks as if he's cutting up more birthday cake. I thought we'd polished it off last night.'

'No one is allowed to leave Iran until the last mouthful has gone.'

I grinned. 'Now that's an invitation for us all to stay if ever there was one.'

At the sound of our laughter, Ali looked up. He didn't exactly scowl, but the icy look he threw me was enough to send a shiver down my spine.

'Catch you later.' I hurried forward to put as much gap between the two of us as possible.

I have no musical talent whatsoever and a museum devoted to traditional Iranian instruments didn't feature high on my list of must-see places. Nonetheless, I dutifully wandered at the tail end of the group as the museum guide led us along the lines of displays of lutes, zither-like instruments and drums, half-listening to her commentary though I will admit that the decoration on some items was worthy of a photo. In its defence, I will say it was one of the best laid out museums I've ever been in. Ultra-modern with clean lines, there was no peering into dark recesses. The light levels were enhanced by white walls and white tiles on the floor. Even the white stands at the base of the glass display cases reflected the light.

At the end of the tour, we were shown into a small room where we were to be treated to a short concert. Once we were seated, our young guide disappeared to inform the musicians we were ready. As soon as she left, Aahil jumped up onto the stage and sat down behind a large zither-like instrument. He picked up a couple of sticks then looked up and grinned. We thought at first, he was just messing about while we waited but then he began to play. He may not have passed his grade eight or whatever the top musical exam grade might be in Iran, but he gave a creditable performance which we all applauded.

He was back in his place by the time the student musicians arrived. It was only a short concert, but the music ranged from haunting and quite moving to jolly – the sort of thing you wanted to clap along to.

Everyone was excited at the prospect of our farewell dinner. Aahil assured us that not only would the food be good – the restaurant had one of the best reputations in the country – but we would also be entertained by a choir while we dined.

When we arrived, we were shown to a large circular table at the side of the room.

'The food has to be good here. Have you seen the number of tables for the locals?' said Paula as she sat down next to me.

There were a couple more conventional large tables on either side of us alongside the wall, but most of the centre of the room was filled with large round raised cushioned areas. In the nearest was a family of six, a couple of teenaged boys and their parents with an older couple. They were reclined around the edge resting against the encircling wooden backrest eating with their fingers from the various dishes laid out in the centre.

'I see what you mean.'

As always happened when we ate as a group, Aahil ordered a mixed selection of dishes to suit everybody's tastes and preferences. Wine flowed freely and the whole room resounded with the hum of convivial chatter and the occasional burst of uninhibited laughter.

Towards the end of the evening, thirty or so singers in colourful garb entered through the far door and mounted the stage which was well over to our left. I could only see it by turning my chair right round but when people started standing up, any chance of getting a decent photo was well and truly scuppered.

They sang lustily for half an hour before the performance came to an end. When I turned back to my table, I noticed that my glass was almost full.

'I could have sworn I only had a thimbleful left,' I muttered to no one in particular.

I'm not much of a wine drinker and I'd only accepted a glass to be sociable. I took a couple of sips, but it was much too dry for my taste. What I really fancied was a coffee but there was no evidence that it was available. There were no waiters in the vicinity, so I picked up my glass of water.

The buzz of conversation continued around me but suddenly, I began to feel quite detached from my surroundings. I ran a finger around the inside of my collar.

'Are you alright, sweetie?'

'I feel a bit faint. I need some fresh air.'

I stood up.

'I'll come with you.'

It wasn't easy weaving my way between the tightly packed tables and how I managed to get to the door without keeling over I'll never know. Once we were in the empty corridor I leant with my back against the wall. Aunt Jessica was never one to make a fuss, thank goodness. She waited patiently until I recovered though I was all too well aware that she never took her eyes from my face.

'Are you okay, Harry?' Paula's voice almost made me jump. I hadn't realised she followed us. 'You went as white as a sheet.'

'A lot better now, thanks,' I managed to mumble.

'It was getting quite hot in there,' she said. 'Would you like me to fetch you some water?'

It was Aunt Jessica who answered. 'That would be kind.'

Paula disappeared back into the dining-room and almost simultaneously Aunt Jessica and I raised eyebrows but neither of us said anything and the girl was back in seconds.

'I snaffled a bottle of mineral water from the bar.'

She handed it to me.

'Thanks.' I struggled to unscrew the cap, so Aunt Jessica took it and did it for me.

I took a sip and leant back against the wall again. 'Actually, I think what I'd really like is to sit down.'

'I'll get you a chair.'

'Please don't!' I managed to stop Paula just as she reached the restaurant door. 'I really don't want any fuss. I'll be fine in a moment or two.'

She frowned then nodded. 'If you say so. But I still think you should sit down before you keel over. Let me just take a look round the corner and see if there's a bench or a chair.'

The decision was taken out of my hands. 'I think that would be a very good idea. I'll stay here and keep an eye on him.'

With both of them ganging up on me, it was pointless to protest. The initial detachment was fading fast, but my legs still felt weak.

There wasn't a bench, but Paula had discovered a large alcove set into the wall and, once the large vase holding an elaborate flower arrangement had been gently pushed to the back, I was able to perch on the edge. The main advantage was that it was out of sight of any diners who decided to pop out to the rest rooms.

'You're missing all the fun,' I said. After all the concern she'd showed, it seemed rude to ask Paula to go but I dearly wished she would.

'Don't worry about that.' She smiled. 'Do you have low blood pressure?'

'No. Why do you ask?'

'It's often the reason people feel faint.'

'This has never happened to me before.'

'Really.' Her eyebrows lifted slightly then gave what I could only call a thoughtful frown. 'Well, if you're sure you'll be okay, I'll pop back.'

'We'll be there in a couple of minutes,' I assured her.

CHAPTER 34

Once I returned to the table, no one remarked on my long absence. I made sure to chat away in the hope that they would assume I'd just popped out to the toilet. To my intense relief, not long after, Aahil announced that it was time we all headed back to the hotel.

'Feeling better?' Aunt Jessica said, when we reached my room.

'Much. I felt really odd. Are you thinking what I'm thinking?'

'That your wine was spiked?'

'I wondered if I was being paranoid. I only took a few sips after my glass had been refilled. Heaven knows what state I'd have been in if I'd polished off the whole glass.'

'The question is who could have slipped something into your drink?'

'Paula was sitting next to me and then Phil and Helen Edwards.'

'We were all watching the show so it could have been anyone. Especially if they came round with a bottle filling glasses. No one notices people acting as waiters.'

'But why? What did they hope to achieve? To poison me?'

Aunt Jessica frowned then shook her head. 'I don't think that the intention was to kill you.'

'Then what?'

'This may sound a little crazy but what if you were given something to make you more compliant, to reduce your inhibitions so they could question you?'

'What about? I don't know anything.'

'Perhaps it's related to you speaking with Yusef's sister. What if whoever killed her was desperate to find out if she'd told you anything? Did you notice anyone in the corridor when you left the restaurant?'

'I wasn't looking.'

'I caught a glimpse of someone coming towards us as I followed you out, but I was more concerned about you. I thought no more about it until now.'

'But who's behind all this?'

'As to who, I've no idea, but I'm beginning to wonder if this could be something to do with politics.'

'Politics!'

'Let's just backtrack a moment. Establish what we know so far. Yusef wanted to see his dying father one last time and was prepared to put his life in danger by coming back to Iran to do so. Those photos were his only insurance.'

'Agreed, but what has that to do with politics?'

'Do you remember when we were in Yazd and we saw all those posters. Aahil told us that the election of the new president is due to take place in a few months' time. I think the man in Yusef's photographs could be one of the candidates. Even if they were taken over forty years ago, photos showing him gambling and womanising would ruin his chances. It wouldn't be just his reputation at stake, it could mean a very long and uncomfortable imprisonment or even execution.'

'But the pictures are just copies. They must have realised he would have left the originals back home. In any case, they were only intended as insurance – a bargaining chip if he was arrested. As far as we know, he never made a direct threat against anyone. All he wanted to do was slip quietly into the country, see his father and return home.' I ran my hands through my hair. 'One thing doesn't make sense in all this. Even if they didn't trust Yusef not to denounce this man, why kill him before they had the photos? His pockets and his room were bound to be searched after his death and the photos discovered.'

'Exactly. Which makes me wonder if Yusef's death was an accident. Before you start protesting, what I'm saying is that the intention wasn't to kill him but to give him a warning. He probably had someone tailing him the moment he arrived in the country. You said yourself, he kept checking behind him all the time. Perhaps the driver was meant to keep an eye on him while he was walking to the ceramic museum to ensure he didn't make contact with anyone he shouldn't. When he saw Yusef on his phone and step into the road he decided to give him a scare. But because Yusef turned at the last moment, the car caught him at the wrong angle, and he was thrown into the path of an oncoming van. That was what killed him, not the car. And, if you think about it, no one could have planned that whole set of circumstances in advance.'

I nodded. 'And once Yusef died, they had no choice but to find those photos.'

'Exactly.'

A dreadful thought suddenly struck me. 'So Yusef's sister's murder and what happened to Hossein Kamali and Irene was what? Collateral damage?'

'Sadly yes. Our would-be president couldn't risk the stick being found by someone else and him being recognised. We know Yusef's room was searched. If you and I suspected that there was something odd going on between Irene and Hossein and that was somehow linked with Yusef, perhaps the spy in our party saw it too. I think when we are able to talk with Hossein, we'll find that he was kidnapped so they could interrogate him about the photos whereabouts.'

'But I doubt anyone else even knows of their existence.'

'Exactly. Which is why Hossein was tortured. When they realised there was nothing he could tell them, he was abandoned somewhere where his injuries would be assumed to be some sort of mugging. I don't suppose they expected him to survive.'

'What about Irene?'

'I presume after that first unsuccessful attempt to get rid of her, a second attempt might be too risky and arouse suspicion.'

'Either that or it's been too difficult to get her on her own ever since.'

'True. One thing is clear though, Harry. You need to be very careful. I'll be with you every step of the way, but I can't follow you into the gents. I wonder if that's where they planned to nobble you this evening at the restaurant.'

'Funny you should say that. It was exactly where I was planning on going when I went out, but though I wanted to splash my face with water and lock myself in a cubicle till that wooziness passed, I had an instinct that I shouldn't. I wasn't at all comfortable perched on that ledge, but I knew it would be a bad idea to go where I'd be alone and vulnerable in that state.'

She chuckled. 'You've developed a strong instinct for self-preservation over the years. But seriously, Harry, take care. Try and stick to unopened bottles of water and fetch your own coffees and the like. Most important of all, no more questioning people, however subtle you think you're being.'

'Yes, Miss.' I grinned.

'I'm serious, Harry. Promise me.'

'I promise.'

CHAPTER 35

The slap of my bare feet on the tiled bathroom floor echoed in the tiny room and made me feel more cut off than ever. Perhaps that's why the unexpected knock made me stop mid-step. It wasn't until I checked through the spy hole in the door that my heart rate began to return to normal.

'Morning, sweetie. I know I'm a bit early, but I just wanted to know how you are after last night.' Aunt Jessica brushed past me and plonked herself down on the bed.

'I was fine until you nearly gave me a heart attack just now.'

She laughed as though I'd made a joke.

'You could have been anyone.'

'You're serious.'

'Knowing you are a target does tend to make you a bit jumpy especially when you have no idea who is out to get you, or where or when.'

'Sorry, Harry. I should have thought and called out or something.'

Jigging about as I stood on one leg trying to put on my sock wasn't the most dignified of positions and I couldn't claim the high ground for long.

'It's okay. I'm fine now.'

'Well on the plus side, we'll be spending most of the day travelling in the coach, so you'll be out of harm's way.'

'There is that.' I knelt down to rescue my trainers from under the desk space below the wall-mounted television.

Probably best not to mention that the idea of being trapped in a confined space with whoever was acting as spy in our party – more than likely the same person who had slipped a Mickey Finn into my drink last night – was a good deal less comforting that she had made it sound. Once I'd tied my shoelaces, I stood up.

'I'm starving. Shall we get something to eat?'

We had no choice about where to sit in the restaurant as a table had been set aside for the whole party. Half a dozen of the others were down there already when we joined them.

'The hotel seems to be buzzing this morning. Is it me, or do the staff seem a bit agitated about something?' I asked as I pulled out the chair next to Gordon.

'I think it's to do with the police who are back in the hotel,' replied Barbara who was sitting opposite.

'Has something else happened?'

'Apparently a whole load of plain-clothes officers arrived with some senior bod all the way from Tehran. They're questioning all the staff who were on duty on the ground floor on Thursday evening when that poor woman died.'

'How the heck did you find that out?'

Barbara gave a smug smile and tapped her nose. 'I talk to people.'

Irene, who was sitting next to her, said, 'Our Barbara has the ability to wheedle all sorts of stuff out of folk before they realise what they're saying. She'd make a good presenter on those early morning TV news programmes where they interview politicians. Instead of coming out with the obvious question she comes at it from the side once she's lulled them into a false sense of security.'

One of the last to join us was Aahil. 'Good morning, everyone. I'm glad I've caught you all. I wanted to let you know there's a slight change of plan. We are going to be leaving half an hour later than planned this morning. I expect we'll make it up easily on the journey so we should be back in Tehran at roughly the time we anticipated.'

'Does that mean the police are going to want to speak to us?' asked Mary.

'As far as I know, they are only interested in the staff who were moving around.' Aahil looked around the table. 'Is everyone here?'

'Paula's not come down yet.'

'She's probably been and gone because we saw her disappearing in the lift as we came out of our room. I expect she went to reception to pay her hotel bill.'

'No problem,' said Aahil. 'I'll ring her room and tell her about the later start.'

It was only when I sat down in my usual window seat halfway down the coach that I realised how tense I'd been simply walking through the lobby, just in case some policeman should decide to stop me and demand a second interview. Wonderful though Isfahan had been, in tourist terms, my favourite city on the trip, I was happy to get underway. Hassan was already sitting in the driver's seat, but Ali was still putting the last of the cases in the hold. I willed him to get a move on.

Paula was the last to appear in the hotel doorway. She handed over her case and climbed aboard. Though most passengers tended to sit in the same places, with so many spare seats available, there was always a bit of changing. The couples often split up so that they could both have a window seat and spread themselves out. It was a moment or two before I realised that Paula had taken the usually empty seat behind me. I told myself firmly there was no cause for alarm. Robert had already moved across the aisle into the single seat where Paula tended to sit and she had simply chosen another.

I squashed the thought that she had been quick to follow me out of the restaurant the previous evening, but she must have seen Aunt Jessica had left with me and realised she had no chance of getting me on my own.

Our first stop was at the small city of Natanz. I can't say I remember much of the journey. I must have been lulled into a doze by the gentle rocking of the coach and the comfortable seat. Aunt Jessica had to give me a gentle nudge when we stopped.

I still wasn't feeling that lively as we walked to the shrine of one of the important Sufi saints and much of Aahil's explanation of how it was Sufis who brought Islam to the town in the fourteenth century went straight over my head.

There was little shade, and the unrelenting sun was still beating down on us by the time we reached the Friday Mosque. After two weeks in the country, I was pretty "mosqued-out", and spent my time taking photos, not even bothering to take in Aahil's commentary.

The town was famous for its pottery, and we went to see an artist hand-painting an elegant looking vase, but I was more than happy to get back to the coach where the two drivers had laid out coffee and biscuits for us on the table alongside.

I stood in the queue waiting for my coffee idly chatting with Aunt Jessica. Once I was handed my plastic cup, I stepped back out of the way only to collide with someone behind me. My cup went flying but most of the contents shot over the ground and not on me or anyone else thank goodness.

'I'm so sorry,' said a crestfallen Paula. 'Here take mine. I haven't started it.'

'It's fine …'

'I insist.' She thrust the cup into my hand and hurried away.

Aunt Jessica had a pensive look as she watched Paula retrieve the fallen cup and hurry over to the bin over by the wall.

'I could be overreacting, but did she deliberately jog my arm?' I asked.

Aunt Jessica took her time before answering. 'You could well be correct.'

I stared at my cup suspiciously. Suddenly, I'd lost my thirst.

Neither of us brought up the subject when we climbed back onto the coach. With no more lectures from Aunt Jessica or contributions from Aahil, the coach fell quiet with most people looking out of the window or gently dozing. Apart from Aunt Jessica and me, the only people sitting together were Barbara and Irene on the front seat. Even they only exchanged the occasional comment. Whether that was because after two weeks they were talked out or were intimidated by the silence, I had no way of telling. All I knew was that this was not the place to discuss private matters.

Not for the first time, taking every member of the party in turn, I went over what I'd discovered about them – even the seemingly-innocent Mary and Gordon, and the ex-teachers Phil and Helen. I had my doubts about Phil. By all accounts he was the only one capable of taking charge after the sight of Yusef's mangled corpse had rendered everyone temporarily felled at the knees. He certainly had the brains, but he had shown little interest in anything else that had been going on.

As Irene had pointed out earlier, Barbara made it her business to find out about everything. On the basis of the least likely person turning out to be the baddie in nearly all the television dramas that are churned out these days, perhaps I should put her on my suspect list, but somehow, I just couldn't picture the bubbly, good-natured woman in the role of a villain. The way she had taken Irene under her wing after the fall surely proved her genuine concern for others. Or did it? What better way was there to find out exactly what Irene knew about what was going on? If Irene had opened up to Aunt Jessica and me, she could well be putty in Barbara's hands.

There again, was Irene really the victim she made herself out to be?

My instincts still put Robert and Paula at the top of my suspect list. I glanced across at Aunt Jessica who had her eyes closed though somehow, I doubted she was sleeping. It suddenly occurred to me – not once had she speculated on who our inside man might be. I'd voiced my doubts about various people, most of which she'd pooh-poohed, but if she had suspicions about anyone in particular, she'd kept them to herself.

After an hour more's driving, we reached Kashan, another oasis town on the main route north. We were taken to Fin Garden, the first of the great Persian gardens built for Shah Abbas I and now recognised by UNESCO. It was pleasantly cool walking alongside the waters of the blue tiled pool under the shade of the tall trees.

As we had come to expect, the two pavilions were filled with stunning architecture and paintings. What made this place more fascinating for most of the party was the story associated with it.

'Amir Kabir served as prime minister to Shah Nasir od-Din. He was a great moderniser and popular with the people. This didn't go down too well at court. Eventually the shah's mother persuaded her son that he had to go. Amir Kabir was imprisoned in the pavilion and eventually murdered in the bath by an assassin sent by the Shah in 1852,' said Aahil as we walked us through the rooms to the bathhouse.

'Well, that was different,' said Mary as we made our way back to coach. 'Anyone know what we're doing for lunch?'

'If it follows the usual pattern, we'll be having a picnic at an old farm.'

'Oh.' Mary's less than enthusiastic expression suggested she wasn't over-impressed with Aunt Jessica's response.

Half an hour later, when the coach pulled off the main highway onto a dirt track road into a dry dusty area, I began to share Mary's reservations. The buildings may have looked rundown, but when we eventually dismounted the coach and were led down to an area alongside a stream and surrounded by trees, it was pleasant enough. There was even a stall selling coffee and snacks on the far side of the water.

Aahil pointed out the locations of the loos at the end of the row of old barns and we all went to explore while he and the drivers prepared our picnic. I took my time looking at some old farm machinery lying around.

'Do you think any of this is still used? It's old but it still looks serviceable.'

'The harvest was over long ago,' Aunt Jessica answered. 'This time of year, I think they open the place to the tour companies as a lunch spot as there is not much else on the main route from Isfahan and Tehran.'

There were no tables and chairs in the picnic area but the stumps of three or four large trees provided large flat surfaces all laid out with mouth-watering fare by the time we returned. Arranged around them were low sawn tree trunks to act as stools.

More patties, tartlets, bowls of dips, tomatoes and salad stuffs, bowls of nuts and enormous dates sat on the small table from the luggage compartment.

'Eat, eat!' urged a smiling Hassan.

'There's enough here to feed an army,' said Caroline. 'We can't possibly get through all this.'

'I should start eating,' said Aahil. 'There's cake, biscuits and fruit to follow.'

CHAPTER 36

'I'm stuffed,' I said as I licked my fingers.

'I'm not surprised,' said Aunt Jessica. 'That must be the sixth of those savoury tarts you've tucked into.'

'Seems such a shame to waste them. I've no idea what was in them, but they were very tasty.'

'Fancy a coffee?'

'I'll get them.' I pushed myself up from the low wall that lay at the top of the bank down to the water. 'Actually, I think I'd prefer a proper coffee with real milk.'

'If you're talking about a coffee from the stall over there, I dare say that's made from milk powder too.'

'Probably. But it tastes better.'

There was a slab bridge across the stream a little further down. I wasn't the only one who'd decided to cross over. Phil and Helen also had the same idea and stood waiting at the stall.

'It's taking a while for the machine to heat up again I think,' said Helen.

We stood chatting for several minutes before they were served, and it was my turn. It was no easy task to walk back along the uneven track down the slope to the bridge and back up with cups filled to the brim without slopping the contents into the saucer.

I handed one to Aunt Jessica and looked straight into her eyes as I said, 'I forgot to get the sugar. I'll leave mine on the end of the wall. Keep an eye on it for me.'

She frowned a little knowing quite well neither of us

took sugar, but she nodded.

I took my time making my way back to the stall, using sign language to point out what I wanted. Lots of people were milling about stretching their legs before the rest of the long drive, by the time I crossed the river back to others.

Tearing off the top of the paper tube of sugar I poured it into the cup and stirred it with the plastic stick I'd been given. I lifted the cup to my lips and pretended to sip. The milky froth formed a moustache above my top lip, and I gave a contented sigh. In my peripheral vision, I saw my aunt wasn't the only one keeping a keen eye on what I was doing. So was Paula. She pulled her phone from a pocket. I turned away, wiped my lip with the back of my hand and began to walk down the slope and slowly downstream.

I didn't plan on going too far. Just a sufficient distance to be out of sight and out of earshot of normal conversation. I found a convenient post to perch on and sat gazing out into the distance wondering how long I'd have to wait.

It took longer than I'd anticipated. I'd almost given up.

'The coach will be leaving soon.'

I turned and gave him a smile. 'Your English is excellent.'

'I speak only a little. It is taught in our schools. Have you enjoyed your stay in my country?'

'Veeery much.'

'This your first time?'

I nodded and grinned like an idiot. 'Wonderful country…people so friendly…generous.'

'They give you gifts?'

Very slowly, I shook my head.

'You give gift to lady?'

'What lady?'

'Lady in hotel. What she tell you?'

'The one in the blue dress?'

He took another step towards me. I must have flinched

because his eyes widened when he realised I'd been faking.

I saw a flash of light from the blade before I'd registered he'd pulled out a knife. I stepped back as he lunged at me, but not quickly enough. I stumbled as I twisted away from him and went down on one knee. As I fell, the blade sliced across my bicep just below my sleeve. Down on the ground, I was helpless. He raised his arm, ready to strike again.

'Stop! Armed police!'

In the brief second it took for him to register the cry from the top of the bank above us, I threw my whole weight at him, knocking him over. We rolled around on the stony path, my hands gripping his wrist, desperately trying to make him drop the knife. After a struggle, he managed to get on top of me and pulled his hand free. This was it. I closed my eyes.

The next thing I knew, he was being pulled off me by a man in black combat gear and there were voices all around me.

I lay there for a few seconds trying to get my breath back before pushing myself up onto the elbow of my good arm. Someone tried to help me up, but I waved them away and sat up to inspect the cut. It stung like crazy and was bleeding steadily, but it wasn't a deep cut and no more than an inch long. More of a nick, though it felt as though Ali had sliced halfway through my arm.

'You'll live.' Aunt Jessica was now kneeling beside me.

'When did you get here?'

She folded a clean handkerchief into a pad and pressed it on my wound as she said, 'I came with Paula.'

'I heard her call out earlier. It's what made Ali hesitate.'

I looked round to find her. She was talking to two policemen though I had no idea where they'd appeared from. Another uniformed officer was keeping a firm hold of the squirming Ali while another tried to handcuff his hands behind his back. I couldn't see Ali's face, but I could hear him cursing.

It took both of the officers to frogmarch him along the path in the opposite direction from the picnic site. He wasn't going to go quietly.

Now that they had gone, Paula turned her attention to me.

'That was a very risky thing to do. You could have been killed.'

I grinned up at her. 'You weren't going to get evidence against him any other way, were you? I've saved what's left of the coffee if you want to test it. Most of it ended up slopped in the saucer.'

She pulled the small scarf from round her neck and knelt down to bind the handkerchief Aunt Jessica was still pressing on my arm. 'How did you work it all out?'

'I realised I'd been drugged last night. If I'm honest, you were my main suspect. It was only when you knocked the cup out of my hand earlier, I realised you had to be one of the good guys stopping me from making the same mistake twice. Was it poison he put in there or an hallucinogenic?'

She gave a low chuckle. 'You're not as green as you're grass-coloured, are you?'

'Why, thank you, ma'am. I think. If you're not the one sent to rub me out, who exactly are you? A backroom researcher and would-be reporter you are not!'

She gave a sheepish grin. 'No. That was just a cover, but explanations will have to wait.' She glanced at her watch. 'We should be getting back to the rest of the party before they start asking questions and someone comes to find us. I promise I will answer all your questions, as far as I can, once we get to the hotel but until then I'd appreciate your discretion. Ali was only one small spoke in the wheel so to speak. The end of this operation is in sight, but not yet complete. I will have a quiet word with Hassan and Aahil now but the less everyone else knows about what's been going on the better.'

I looked down at my blood-soaked T-shirt and gave a snort. 'And you think they're not going to realise something's happened when they see me in this state!'

'You have a point.' She thought for a minute. 'I'll go back and tell Aahil and Hassan what's happened and fetch you a clean T-shirt. In the meantime, you can make your way back and clean yourself up in the loo. There's a path along the top of the bank that runs through the wood to the back of the farmyard. Jessica will show you. That's the way we followed you, keeping out of sight.'

'Good idea,' said Aunt Jessica. 'And can you get Hassan to give you the medical kit? It will have something we can dress this with properly.'

'Good idea. We can tell everyone you were walking in the woods and got a small cut when you tripped over a tree root. It should distract everyone from realising Ali's no longer with us.'

'Won't they have already suspected something when they saw two black cars drive into the farmyard and four burly officers burst out of the doors? Never mind when they spot Ali being carted off.'

Paula's tinkling laugh rang out. 'I should have realised you'd spotted the cars following us. But in answer to your question there's more than one way into this place. There's a second track at the far end of the farm.'

CHAPTER 37

Our flight back to Heathrow the next morning was at midday but because we needed to check in three hours beforehand, it made much more sense to stay at a hotel close to the airport rather than the Palace Hotel in the centre of the city where we had stayed before.

'It is literally a five-minute walk from the hotel across the foot bridge to the airport doors if you are happy to carry all your luggage. But if you prefer to use the hotel's courtesy bus you are welcome to do so. There is a bus every fifteen minutes and it's a ten-minute drive so do check with the hotel and make sure you leave plenty of time. When we arrive, I will check you all in as usual but then I shall be leaving you.'

Phil had been elected as the group's spokesperson and after his vote of thanks to Hassan, Aahil and to Aunt Jessica and much clapping, everyone trooped into the hotel.

'It was really odd Ali leaving us like that and in the middle of nowhere,' said Barbara as we all sat waiting in the lobby for our room keys.

'Didn't Aahil say something about him being collected by a friend he was going to be staying with?' said Caroline.

'But he didn't even say goodbye,' Barbara persisted.

Robert gave a snort. 'That's hardly a surprise. He never said much to anyone while he was with us. Miserable sort of chap if you ask me.'

'You would,' muttered Gordon sotto voce. Seems I

wasn't the only one who would not be sorry to see the back of our transatlantic companion.

'He was very shy and besides I don't think he spoke any English,' said Irene.

I wondered if she would have been so keen to leap to his defence had she realised he was the one who had pushed her down the stairs.

Aunt Jessica managed to find a porter to help carry all the projector equipment and the rest of the hand luggage up to our rooms. I'd slept most of the rest of the afternoon in the coach and felt much more my normal self, but Aunt Jessica was insistent that I didn't lift anything even with my good arm in case it started bleeding again.

Our hotel was typical of the modern concrete and glass buildings that can be found next to almost all international airports, but my room had one big advantage. A large, deep bathtub.

I gently lowered myself into the hot water with a satisfied sigh. I looked down the length of my aching body. I was covered in bruises that seemed to darken and grow in the heat of the water. I'd have dearly loved to have sunk down with only my head above the water, but I couldn't let my bandage get wet. I tried resting my forearm across the top of my head and then on the rim of the tub, but I couldn't get comfortable in any position. Reluctantly, after ten minutes, I climbed out and began the painful job of drying myself virtually one-handed. Not an easy task.

Despite all the care I'd taken, I still managed to get my bandage wet at the edges. Not that it really mattered. Aunt Jessica insisted on inspecting the cut to see if it needed stitches.

'At least the blood washed out any dirt from the wound. It's still oozing a little, but no need to cart you off to hospital.'

She dabbed antiseptic cream onto the central pad of a large band aid plaster and strapped it on.

By the time I'd put on a long-sleeved shirt and tucked it to a pair of cleanish jeans, and combed my hair, I decided I looked sufficiently presentable. My trainers were a bit scruffy, but I couldn't be bothered to give them a good scrub.

'If you've finished admiring yourself in that mirror, it's time we were going. We're already two minutes late,' said Aunt Jessica, smiling at me.

We'd arranged to meet in Paula's room where there was no fear of our conversation being overheard.

'Come on in. Make yourselves comfortable. Would either of you like a drink before we start? Something from the minibar or there's tea or coffee?'

Irene had beaten us to it and was already sitting on the double settee by the picture window. Aunt Jessica sat down next to her, leaving me to make myself comfortable on the side of the bed facing them.

As our host went to fill the kettle in the ensuite, Irene said, 'Paula's just been telling me about your little adventure at lunch-time.'

'I'm not quite sure that's how I would describe it,' I said. 'But I'm relieved it's all over.'

'But is it all over? I'm so confused. I'm not quite sure what's been happening.'

'I'm sure we all have lots of questions, Irene,' interrupted Paula. 'That's why I invited you all here. I thought we could piece the whole thing together.'

Paula handed out the drinks – cups of tea for Irene and Aunt Jessica, a lemonade for me and tonic water for herself, then sat beside me on the bed.

'Perhaps it's best if I start and explain a little about how I fit in to all this. As you have probably worked out by now, I work for the security services and my department is working with various international agencies through INTERPOL. There is obviously a limit as to how much I can reveal but as all three of you have been dragged into this operation, I believe it's only fair I give you some explanation. The man you know as Yusef Kaya has been a person of interest to my department for some time.'

'Or as I knew him forty years ago, Reza Darbandi,' said Irene.

'Exactly. Once we knew he was coming to Iran, I was sent to observe. What you might not know, is that Reza blotted his copybook as far as his loyalty to the regime was concerned when your then fiancé Mahmoud slipped through SAVAK's fingers. Whether Reza actually helped get him out of the country we'll probably never know, but his failure to report Mahmoud's disappearance until the next morning left him vulnerable, and the only way he could redeem himself was to agree to plead guilty to a smuggling charge to protect the son of a prominent member of the Shah's inner circle caught with a considerable stash of heroin.'

Irene nodded. 'Hossein discovered that he'd been in prison.'

'Deals to protect wayward young men and women belonging to extended royal families were not uncommon in that part of the world, though usually it was loyal subjects who volunteered to do the time rather than like Reza who appears to have been blackmailed into it. Reza spent sixteen years in jail in return for a substantial sum and a new life in Turkey. He also negotiated a deal for his family. They were spared the shame of his imprisonment by being given new identities and moved to Isfahan.'

'So what went wrong?' I asked. 'Why was his life in danger if he returned to Iran to see his dying father? Even if it was made a condition of the original deal that he never set foot in the country that was forty odd years ago, when a different regime was in power. Why would the authorities be bothered now?'

'We believe that the man who actually committed the offence is now a prominent official in government and destined for even higher things. Any scandal at such a crucial time when things are on a knife-edge in the Middle East might destabilise the current regime.'

'So was Reza blackmailing them by threatening to reveal the story?' I asked.

'All their plans could be jeopardised if Reza revealed what he knew,' Irene agreed.

Paula shook her head. 'I doubt if he made a direct threat. The real culprit's name was never made public though I don't deny Reza may well have had a good idea as to his identity. As far as we can determine, the problem was that the Iranians began to suspect Reza of being a loose cannon. The fact that he decided to return to Britain a few years ago and meet up with some of his old cronies from his time in London caused a degree of disquiet, but the real crunch came when he broke the original conditions by making contact with his family again. Knowing his father was dying, he was desperate to return home and see him for one last time. That's when he started looking around to find something to act as leverage in case he was discovered.'

'I don't understand,' said a confused-looking Irene. 'Why couldn't he simply threaten to tell his story? Why wasn't that enough?'

'I'm not so sure it was quite that simple. If Reza went to the media with the story that he did time for this man, he would need to produce some pretty substantial evidence that that was the case. After all, he had admitted the charge and served the sentence. Besides which, he gave no indication that he was planning on doing so or that he was even interested in today's Iranian politics.'

'How could they be sure of that?'

'We know that one of his London so-called friends was still loyal to Iran and, with the help of a financial inducement, reported anything suspicious back to Tehran. The first alarm bells came when Reza said he was planning on going back home to see his father before he died.'

'So why not send someone to get rid of Reza straight

away? Why wait for him to come to Iran before they killed him?' I asked.

'We can only assume because they didn't know what evidence he'd found or where it was. They couldn't even be sure if he had it. On another occasion when he was talking about his forthcoming trip, he admitted he was still waiting for the evidence though he refused to answer any of his friend's questions about what it was.'

'We know Reza's hotel room was searched in Tehran. He had a set-to with Mr Kamali about it,' said Aunt Jessica. 'Presumably that was what they were looking for.'

'But why kill him before they had it?' I asked.

'Hossein told me Reza had given him a package to put in the hotel safe. Perhaps they thought that was it and had him killed before he discovered it was missing,' suggested Irene.

Paula nodded. 'Possibly. We know two men claiming to be police had already been to the hotel before our people arrived. But obviously whatever was in the safe couldn't have been it. Why else were you pushed down the stairs, Hossein kidnapped, and Harry drugged?'

'And his poor sister murdered,' I added.

'But if they don't have it, where is this vital piece of insurance Reza had obtained?' asked Irene.

I pulled out the USB stick and handed it over to Paula. 'I think you'll find this could be it. I found it two days ago stuffed down the back of the seat on the coach where Yusef used to sit.'

Her eyes widened. After a moment's hesitation, she seized it from my hand then went to her laptop on the table below the wall-mounted television. She already had it open and fired up so all she had to do was plug in the stick.

The rest of us crowded behind her, staring at the screen as she sank down on the stool.

'I take it that's the man you're talking about?' I asked. 'The one Reza went to prison for now destined for higher things.'

I wasn't surprised when she didn't answer. I hadn't really expected her to.

'Assuming this is what Reza planned to give his sister as a backup to keeping her family safe, it wouldn't have been much use to the those desperate to protect the man's reputation. Reza would have stored away the originals safely back in England where they couldn't be found,' I said.

'You're making the assumption that Reza had them in the first place.'

'If he didn't take the photos, who did?' asked Aunt Jessica. 'Presumably they thought it might be Hossein. Is that why he was kidnapped?'

'I think that could well be the case though the fact that they let him go, suggests that he knew nothing about them or even what Reza was up to,' said Paula. 'Though that might well explain why Ali pushed you down the stairs when he heard you take a call from Hossein.'

'So if it wasn't Reza or Hossein who took the photos, who did? It had to be someone in London at the time they were all students there together,' asked Irene.

'Mahmoud,' Aunt Jessica's voice was barely more than a whisper.

Paula twisted round to face her.

'That would be my guess. He could never have appreciated the heights to which his fellow student might rise one day but knowing the disgrace those photos would bring to the boy's father who was one of the Shah's leading advisors, Mahmoud realised their importance. The threat of making those photos public would ensure the boy's co-operation in Mahmoud's plans to stay in Britain. Perhaps they were the leverage Mahmoud used to ensure Reza waited for him to escape before informing SAVAK of his disappearance. Unless we manage to track down Mahmoud himself, we'll probably never know.'

'So what happens now?'

'As far as you three are concerned, nothing. This business is over. Ali is now in custody, and you are free to go home.'

She unplugged the USB stick and closed down her laptop.

'But what about Hossein?' asked Irene.

'I spoke to my colleague when we first arrived here. Hossein is doing well. He's fully conscious now though still very groggy and confused. As far as the doctors can ascertain, he was heavily drugged, and they'll be keeping him in hospital for another day or so just for observation. He was given some sort of hallucinogenic that leaves you awake but highly suggestible. I expect when the analysis comes back, it's the same thing Ali put in your coffee at lunch, Harry.'

'Presumably the same stuff he put in my wine at the farewell dinner?' I said bitterly.

'Exactly. When no one followed you out, I wondered if they could be waiting for you outside. I didn't see anyone out there but presumably with Jessica by your side, they disappeared. I was worried someone could be waiting in the men's toilets'

'Is that why you fetched water and found him somewhere to sit?' Aunt Jessica asked.

Paula nodded.

'That's when I decided you must be one of the good guys after all,' Aunt Jessica said.

'I beg your pardon?' Paula's eyes widened.

'Harry and I knew from the start that Yusef, as we knew him then, didn't die from any accidental hit-and-run. It looked like he was deliberately mown down, though why we still have no idea.'

Paula looked at me suspiciously. 'I began to suspect you must have worked that out especially when you started asking me odd questions. I guessed you and Jessica knew a great deal more than you were saying. Once it became clear you were keeping a close eye on Irene, I still wasn't sure whose side you were on.'

Aunt Jessica and I exchanged glances. 'Harry and I decided much the same thing about there being an inside man.'

'Or woman,' I added pointedly.

Paula laughed. 'And I was on top of your list?'

'Not quite, but a close second.'

'I don't know about you three, but I'm beginning to feel peckish.' Irene glanced at her watched. 'I promised Barbara I'd meet her for dinner in half an hour, so if you'll excuse me, I must be going, but before I do, I just want to say a big thankyou to you all for sorting everything out and particularly to Jessica and Harry for looking after me so well.'

'Don't mention it. We'll see you later.'

Once Irene had left, Aunt Jessica turn to Paula. 'You're more than welcome to join us for dinner, if you'd like.'

'I would. Thank you very much.'

CHAPTER 38

The excitement for the day wasn't over.

We had decided to eat in the café area on the ground floor. Apart from not being particularly hungry, I couldn't face the thought of having to smarten up and get changed yet again to go to the main restaurant. The realisation of my folly in attempting to tackle Ali on my own was only now beginning to sink in and I was feeling thoroughly knackered.

The café was more of an extension to the corridor than a proper room, with small tables lined up along the walls with a counter area at the end. I pulled a chair from a nearby table so the three of us could sit together.

'There's not much of a choice,' said Aunt Jessica studying the menu. 'Beef or cheeseburger and chips, a couple of varieties of pizza or soup of the day. There's a selection of filled baguettes if you're not fussy about having something hot.'

I hadn't bothered to look round to see if any others in our party had had the same idea before I sat down, but I recognised her voice the moment I heard it.

'...I've had enough of your lame excuses. I don't believe you, you lying bastard.'

We all turned to see what was happening.

They were sitting a good thirty feet away and Robert had his back to us, and his voice was low, so we couldn't hear his reply. But it clearly wasn't enough to convince his wife.

Caroline pushed her chair away and stood up. I could see her knuckles turn white as she gripped the edge of the table. As she turned to storm out of the room, he seized her arm. 'It's not what you think. I promise you.'

'Then prove it. Show me your phone.'

When he hesitated, she pulled her arm away and for a moment it looked as though she was about to slap him across the face. He leant back in the chair making it rock precariously on its two back legs.

Seizing the opportunity, she grabbed at the mobile lying on the table and dunked it into the jug of water.

'You stupid woman!'

Pulling up his sleeve, Robert plunged his hand into the jug. Had the atmosphere not been so tense, it might have been funny to watch him. With the phone clenched in his hand, there was no way he could pull it out of the narrow neck of the jug. In the end, he upended the water over the table, grabbed the mobile and ran after his wife who was now long gone.

All chatter in the café had stopped. The only sound was the obligatory background muzak. Only after a good thirty seconds did the low hum of conversation resume again.

'What do you make of that?' I asked. 'Sounds as though our gallant American has been playing away. I knew he was up to something.'

Paula looked thoughtful.

'Do you know something we don't?' asked Aunt Jessica.

At first, Paula's blank stony face suggested she was not going to let on, but she hadn't reckoned on Aunt Jessica.

'I'm guessing those phone calls weren't from a mistress but with something else altogether. A business deal, perhaps? From the way he was trying to keep quiet about it, even from his wife, I take it that it was not exactly legal. Drug related?'

Paula's lips twitched.

'Ahh. So all that talk of heroin you spun Harry was

merely to send us looking in the wrong direction.'

Paula held up her hands in submission. 'I can see you are going to keep pestering.' She took a quick look round to check that we couldn't be overheard. 'After Reza's unexpected death, the Department did a preliminary search into the backgrounds of everyone on the tour and Robert Morrison quickly became a person of interest.'

'Caroline told me,' I said, 'he was a business consultant and spent most of his working life in the Middle East.'

'It's true that at one stage he worked for an American company with interests in this part of the world, but he acquired a gambling habit. After systematically fiddling his expenses for years to pay for his habit he eventually overreached himself. Not long after he was fired, he moved to Cleveland and managed to find himself a rich widow ten years older than himself and became a kept man. That is until the money ran out three years ago and he skipped the marriage and came to Britain.'

'And tried the same trick on poor Caroline. I wonder if she knows he's a bigamist.'

'Bet I'm not the only one dying to know what happened last night,' I said to Aunt Jessica as we made our way down to breakfast the next morning.

She gave me a disapproving frown.

'Admit it. You're just as eager to find out as I am but are just too polite to admit it.'

Her lips twitched. 'You may have a point.'

'I may have been wrong about Robert being involved with what was happening to Irene and Hossein, but I was convinced there was something not quite kosher about him.'

The lift stopped and two hotel guests joined us, so I was spared any caustic comment about me also suspecting nearly every other person in our party.

I held open the restaurant door for her. As she gave our names and room numbers to the girl sitting at the desk just inside the door, I glanced round the room to see who was already there.

'Caroline is sitting with Barbara and Irene over in the corner, but I can't see Robert anywhere,' I said softly as we trailed after the young waiter who was showing us our assigned table.

Once we were sat down and had a chance to look round, I spotted Phil and Helen at a table with Gordon and Mary. Helen turned and waved but we were too far apart to chat.

'Can't see Robert anywhere, can you?'

'For goodness' sake, behave. I'm sure we'll find out all the details eventually so let's have breakfast in peace. I'm going to get us some tea, do you want to find yourself something from the buffet table? It's going to be a long day and we won't be back home till late.'

I'm not much of one for a big, cooked breakfast but aircraft meals are never brilliant, so I decided to go for the Iranian equivalent of the Full English. I finished off the last mouthful of the watery scrambled egg and pushed away my empty plate. I was tossing up whether to investigate the bread and pastry counter when I heard someone coming up behind me.

'Good morning to you both.'

'Hi, Mary. How are you?'

'Sad it's all over of course, though I'm not sure that I've the energy to do much more. It's certainly been an eventful holiday, but I just wanted to come over to say thank you, Jessica, just in case I don't get the chance later. Having all those extra insights into the country and your stories about those Shahs and what they got up to helped to put everything in context.'

Aunt Jessica pulled out the empty chair and waved her to sit down. 'Have you enjoyed it?'

'We've seen some amazing places. It really has been the holiday of a lifetime even if there were a couple of upsets.'

'It has been somewhat eventful,' Aunt Jessica answered.

I stifled the instinct to add my two-penny worth.

'You can say that again! Did you hear what happened last night? We heard someone shouting and banging on the door just down the corridor from us. We looked out and it was Robert. Caroline had locked him out. She'd put his case outside the door. The hoo-ha went on for a good ten minutes before it all quietened down. Helen was saying just now she was in the café last night when the two of them had an argument.'

'Oh dear.'

Ignoring Aunt Jessica's comment, Mary hurried on. 'No one seems to know what happened to him. Heaven knows where he slept last night, and he hasn't been seen this morning.'

'I expect he'll be at the airport. Perhaps the two of them might have made it up by then.'

If Mary was disappointed by Aunt Jessica's calm reception of her news, she didn't show it. 'I'd better be getting back to the others. They'll be wondering where I am.'

'Do you really think Caroline will have him back?' I asked once Mary had left.

Aunt Jessica shrugged. 'Who knows? We'll just have to wait and see. Now if you are going to have anything else to eat, I suggest you go and take a look now. The flight might not be until this afternoon, but we do have to check-in three hours before hand, and we're supposed to vacate our rooms by ten. I don't suppose you're anywhere near finished packing either, knowing you.'

'Almost,' I lied. She knew me too well.

EPILOGUE

Three weeks later

Christmas lights glittered from shop windows as we drove north through the crowded streets towards the M11. Lines of snowflake shapes and tiny angels strung low across the street flickered above making it even more difficult to read the road signs. Four-thirty on a Friday evening in mid-December wasn't the best time to be heading out of London.

'Christmas seems to get earlier every year,' moaned Aunt Jessica. 'I'll swear they start decorating the shops the moment the summer sales are over. I've still not found the time to write the last of my Christmas cards yet.'

'Well let's face it, there was no time to give it much thought before we went to Iran and things have been pretty full-on since we've come back.'

'You can say that again,' she said with feeling.

'Talking of our holiday, I wonder what happened to Robert. We saw most of the rest of the party when we walked over from the hotel, but even when we changed planes at Istanbul, I never spotted him.'

'That's hardly surprising. The timing was so tight, we were too busy getting to our gate to worry about anyone else.'

'True, but I can't help wondering if they sat next to each other in the plane or if Caroline managed to change her seat.'

'Possibly. We'll never know, but right now we're moving off again so keep your eyes on the car in front.'

Minutes later, we ground to a halt for the umpteenth time and watched the lights change from green to red a couple more times before our car reached the front.

Things became much easier once we hit the motorway, but the traffic was heavy even when we turned onto the A11 and began heading towards Newmarket.

'I know she says she's fine, but Maud isn't getting any younger and I feel guilty I've left it so long. I know you've been inundated with work ever since, but just because you had to cancel our visit at the last minute there's no valid reason I couldn't have caught the train and gone up by myself.'

'We're here now, at least we will be in an hour's time.'

Almost as soon as I pulled up in front of the gate, the front door was thrown open and my mother stood there, arms wide and with a great smile on her face.

'You go straight in,' I said to Aunt Jessica. 'I'll bring the luggage.'

I stepped out of the car, gave my mother a wave and went to the boot.

Aunt Jessica was already in the front room by the time I'd brought in everything.

'My goodness, what's all this?' said my mother after I'd been enveloped in a bear hug.

'I brought the screen and the projector so I can show you all our photos. I'll pop it out of the way in the dining-room for now if that's alright.'

'Of course it is. Then go and say hello to Maud. She's been so looking forward to your visit. The kettle's on. I'll just go and make some tea.'

I smiled weakly at her departing figure. The only reason why my fearsome Aunt Maud would be pleased to see me was because she'd had no one to intimidate for a while. Plastering on my best smile, I pushed open the front room door and went in.

'Hello, there. How are you, Aunt? You look well compared with last time I saw you, I must say.'

'I'm fine. I don't suppose you've brought me any more of those biscuits you made for me in hospital, have you?'

I wasn't sure if she was serious or not. It was difficult to tell with Aunt Maud.

'Er, no. We have brought lots of little biscuits and sweets from Iran though. They are very tasty. I've also brought all the ingredients to make us all a special lunch tomorrow. Aunt Jessica and I decided you might prefer that to us taking you out for a meal in Norwich. It is quite a long journey to the city, and it would be a bit of a squash in the car for five of us.'

'Good idea, though as it happens Edwina's not here. Patricia invited her to stay with her for her school's Christmas end of term celebrations. There was a play of some sort yesterday and it's the carol concert tonight. She's going to stay for the weekend, but you'll see them both on Sunday morning when Patricia brings her back.'

'That's good,' said Aunt Jessica. 'We've brought back a few trinkets for her from our trip.'

My mother arrived with the tea.

'I want to hear all about your adventures,' said my mother. She sat back and let Aunt Jessica describe all the wonderful places we'd seen.

'Persepolis must have been very special. We saw a fascinating programme on the television about it while you were out there. I'm really looking forward to seeing your photos of it.'

'It was wonderful, but I think my favourite city was Isfahan.'

'It's such a good thing you left when you did though. All the trouble they've been having since you arrived back with all these demonstrations about the increase in the price of petrol. It said in the paper the poor finance minister has had to resign over it.'

'We never saw any of that when we were there,' said Aunt Jessica quickly, but any attempt to stem my mother's flow was in vain.

'They said that he was one of the leading candidates in the election for the next president.'

'Really? To be honest I haven't had much time to follow the news since I've been home,' I lied, curbing every instinct to catch Aunt Jessica's eye. The Iranian hierarchy must have been relieved that the petrol riots provided a convenient excuse for the stepping down of their man after the Western Powers had applied pressure using Reza's insurance photos. 'Did I tell you I've just taken on this big new project for a local boutique? They are planning on going into the online market and need to update their whole image and advertising strategy.'

My ploy worked for a time but when my mother brought up the subject again, I had to find another diversion.

'It's about time I took our cases upstairs. Can't leave them cluttering up the hall.'

My mother followed me out.

'I presume Aunt Jessica will be sharing your room as usual?'

'Yes dear. Let me go ahead and open the doors for you.'

It was easier to carry the cases up one at a time as the stairs were quite narrow and my life would not have been worth living if I'd marked the wallpaper or scratched the bannisters. My mother's room overlooked the back garden. I put the case on the spare bed ready for my aunt to unpack.

'I can see to the rest, Mum.' I opened the door to the box room but there was no camp bed.

'No, dear. Not in there. You can sleep in Edwina's room.'

'But...'

'That's why she's staying an extra night with Patricia so you can have the spare bed in here. As Maud said, you're not a child anymore. There's barely room for the camp bed with all that stuff in there anyway.'

'Aunt Maud said that?'

She nodded. 'Do make sure you thank Edwina when you see her. She wasn't at all pleased with the idea but as I pointed out, Maud was quite right, and it wasn't as if you'd be sleeping in her actual bed.'

I left her in the room and went down to the hall to retrieve my grip.

I stood for several moments in the doorway of Edwina's room. I'd never been inside before. It was the largest of the three bedrooms but unlike my mother's, it was crammed with ornate mahogany furniture. The large dressing-table stood in front of the window cutting out much of the light. Victorian in style, it had three mirrors and little drawers in the top on either side. Inevitably, it was cluttered with a variety of bottles, jars and paraphernalia.

The spare bed had been tucked in alongside the wardrobe for Edwina's daughter, Patricia's occasional visits. Much as I dreaded that uncomfortable camp bed with the ever-present threat of the boxes piled up alongside falling down on me in the night, invading Aunt Edwina's territory was a daunting prospect. What felt even more disconcerting was Aunt Maud's apparent mellowing towards me. I knew where I was when everything I tried to do earned her disapproval. Still there was a whole weekend to go yet. No doubt, I'd be back in the doghouse before we left.

Printed in Great Britain
by Amazon